Bob Moats

I0567409

STRIP CLUB
MURDERS

Copyright © 2014 by Bob Moats.

Rev. 0331142030

1

Strip Club Murders

ISBN -978-0-9960845-5-0

For information and address:
Magic 1 Productions
P.O. Box 524, Fraser MI 48026-0524
Website: http://murdernovels.com
Cover by Bob Moats
Stock photo from Fotosearc.com

Bob Moats

Other Jim Richards series books by Bob Moats

(In Series Order)
Classmate Murders
Vegas Showgirl Murders
Dominatrix Murders
Mistress Murders
Bridezilla Murders
Magic Murders
Strip Club Murders
Made-for-TV Murders
Mystery Cruise Murders
Talk Show Murders
Sin City Murders
Black Widow Murders
Vegas Vigilante Murders
Area 51 Murders
Mortuary Murders
Hypnotic Murders
Sunshine State Murders
Blue Suede Murders
Honky Tonk Murders
Dark Carnival Murders
Lipstick Murders
Pasta Murders
Talent Show Murders
Shyster Murders
Campground Murders
Network Murders
Reunion Murders
Big Apple Murders
Kennel Murders
Trick or Treat Murders
Santa Murders
Wiseguy Murders

For a preview or to purchase a book, go to
http://murdernovels.com

What a few people are saying about Murder Novels by Bob Moats

Mr. Moats, I just got your novel "Classmate Murders" and have to let you know, I read it in one evening. That is the first book I have ever done that with. That was the most enjoyable book I have ever read. I just started reading e-books, and reading again, after getting my wife a Kindle. This book was my 12th, and the best. I just got Las Vegas Showgirls to (read) tomorrow evening. I look forward to reading many of your books in this series. I have been searching for an author and books that were fun, entertaining reads. Your books are just the ticket.

Regards, A new fan, Bill from South Carolina

****

Another very nice comment submitted through my website from Micki P.:

"I recently was given a kindle for my 60th birthday. The first book I downloaded was the Classmate Murders and have now read every one of the them. Today I started on the Fatal Rejection series. Thank you for the wonderful ride with Jim and Penny and all the rest of the troop. I have laughed and giggled thru the stories, my poor family gave me the strangest looks! Now I really want a little Yorkie!! Fatal Rejection so far is another great read! I will be looking out for more of Jim Richards and since you are my #1 Author, anything of yours I can find."

****

"I got up to chapter ten of the Classmate Murders and decided then to buy the next two books." ... "Just finished your third book, the Dominatrix Murders. I thought it was the best one of the three, didn't want to put it down till I finished it. I looked forward to see how Penny would greet (Jim) every day after her show. Keep the books coming can't wait for the next one." A. Norris, former Naval Corpsman

Extra special thanks to:

Thank you to all the people who purchased this book. I hope you enjoy it as much as I enjoyed writing it for my faithful readers.

The Jim Richards Family of Readers is listed in the back of the book.

Strip Club Murders
By Bob Moats

Chapter 1

It was dark but I could see. My eyes were closed but I could see. I saw the love of my life, Penny, on my right, sitting by my hospital bed holding my hand. I couldn't feel it. I saw Buck sitting in his usual stretched out position on a chair to my left. I wanted to kick at his feet as I always did to him in my office lobby, but my legs wouldn't move. Matter of fact, I couldn't move any part of my body. I was lying on the bed and I had no idea why I was there, and why Penny and Buck were starting to fade out. I could hear a small sound coming from my right, it was a beeping noise, like you hear in those hospital shows where the patient was hooked up to a heart monitor. Was I hooked up to a heart monitor and was that noise coming from my vitals? The room was getting darker now and the beeping was starting to fade as well.

It was cold and totally dark now, but I started to remember, I could start to see where it all began.

Mornings in my office was generally a time for quiet, I would check my computer for emails, then open the snail mail that arrived the day before, I hadn't been in my office to greet the mail-person. I say mail-person because I'm not trying to be politically correct, but it changed every so often, a male one day, female the next, I never knew what gender it would be. Okay, I was being politically correct; it was built into me to be politically correct. I wasn't happy with my DNA at times, but I learned to accept it.

I hadn't seen Buck in about two weeks, since he went out to visit Maria in Las Vegas. It was kind of lonely without him. Before he went out to Vegas, we had just came back from our adventures out in Colon, Michigan where we went for the magic convention, and got caught up in magic and murder. It was there that we had met Vicky, the widow of the murdered magician Fred, she was a friend now and Penny and Vicky talked every so often on the phone since she lived across the state in Grand Rapids. Penny and I bought Vicky a Toy Yorkie, just like our Willy, to be a companion for her since her husband's death. She loved her pup, and would frequently call Penny for advice on taking care of the dog. I think she also called to hear a friendly voice, too.

I hadn't had a new client in about a week; since returning, I had a couple spousal spying jobs and one background check on a new employee some company had asked for. I wasn't making a lot of money, but between the finder's fee from the mistress murder and the inheritance from my late friend Marty, I really didn't have to work, but I enjoyed the job. Penny would rather I stayed home and took care of Willy, but I knew I couldn't. Not that I didn't want to take care of Willy, but I had to be doing something out of the house just to keep me alive. Penny was concerned about me being shot, and I would joke about her finally getting my money if I was shot. She didn't think it was funny.

I turned on the new 42-inch LCD TV I had put in my office to watch Penny's talk show, and also to give me something to do on boring days. Penny's show hadn't started yet and out of 125 channels I ended up watching a History Channel show on the origins of the National Parks of the U.S., it was interesting. Peter Coyote, the actor, was the narrator, I had to listen really hard to figure out who it was, he did sound a lot like Henry Fonda. I cheated and went to my computer and Googled the show to see who the host was.

I spun in my squeaky desk chair and looked out my office window onto Garfield Road; traffic was light today. It was early, just after the morning rush to work and just before the lunch rush. I spun back to change the channel on the TV to the cartoon network and watched my favorite character, Bugs Bunny. The cartoon running at the moment, had Bugs dressed in women's clothing to throw off Elmer Fudd, Bugs dressed in women's clothing a lot I noticed. I wondered about Bugs.

I shut the TV off, I still had an hour before Penny's show would start, and I sat back thinking about playing Mah Jong tiles on my desktop computer, when my phone rang. I answered with my best "Richards Investigations, how may I help you?", and a rather gravelly voice said, "Mr. Richards?"

"Yes, it is I, Jim Richards at your disposal." I was feeling giddy right about now.

"Mr. Richards, dis is Angelo, from when we met in Vegas." The gruff voice was now recognizable. Angelo was an enforcer for the Traviano mob family who helped me a great deal with tracking down the Bridezilla killer out in Vegas, when Penny and I got married out there.

"Angelo, how the hell are you?" I asked.

"I'm good. I hope I ain't bothering you right now?" he asked.

"No, I'm just sitting here going over my cases." I lied. "Are you calling from Mississippi?"

"No, after Francis married don Traviano out in Vegas, we all moved back to New York, we're set up real nice now."

Strip Club Murders

"That's great, what can I do for you?"

"I still had da card ya gave me when ya offered me a job." He was grinning, I could tell.

"You looking for work Angelo, is family business slow for you now?" I hoped he didn't take offense to the family reference.

"Nah, I was wondering if you could help me this time."

"Angelo, you did good for me in Vegas and I owe you a couple of favors, what is it you need?" I asked.

He paused, I wasn't sure if he was afraid to ask or just trying to get his brain in gear. "I gotta relative out in Detroit, he needs some help and he don't want to involve da cops or da family. He needs to keep it private, I thought of you."

"What is it he needs?"

"Well, he runs a small strip club down around da Detroit border and one of his goils came up missing. He needs someone on da outside to find her. It's complicated. He don't want me involving my connections with da family in Detroit either, wants ta keep it on da QT."

"I see, do you have a number I can call him at?" I asked.

"Nah, he'd rather come to your office, no phone calls, he don't trust no phones."

"Okay, you have my address on the card, have him come in and we'll talk."

"Hey, Mr. Richards, I appreciate da help. You is good people. I let him know to talk with youse." He said good-bye and hung up.

I thought, strip club, Buck would be disappointed he wasn't here.

I turned on the TV again and watched Bugs some more, up until Penny's show came on. She had a couple of kids on her show talking about science experiments that they created for a science fair at a local school. They proceeded to blow up a couple of things with just the power of baking soda and then they made a paper-mache volcano erupt all over the stage. After Penny thanked the children and sent them off, she introduced a man who tested all those products you see advertised on TV. He demonstrated the ones he brought with him and gave his ratings as to their usefulness. It was interesting to see some fail his tests and some even passed.

The show ended and I flipped around the channels and found nothing worth watching, so I shut it off. I went to the couch and relaxed until my door opened and in walked a rather rough looking biker type. Tats all up and down his arms flowing up his neck and he was wearing a black Harley t-shirt with the sleeves ripped off to show off the elaborate tattoos. His arms looked like a soccer team could play on them; they were huge. He had one of those Fu Manchu mustaches and his hair was pulled back to a ponytail that ran down to his belt.

"Hello, are you Jim Richards?" He spoke clearly and enunciated his words carefully. He had a very nice radio announcer type voice, deep and booming, sounding like he had some voice training.

I said I was, and stood to greet him. "You were sent by Angelo?" I asked.

"Yes, sir, I was. He praises you highly, and when Angelo speaks I listen." He was smiling now and had a nice set of choppers, the teeth, not the cycle.

"Please sit." I directed him to the client chair and he sat. I went to my desk chair, sat and leaned forward on my desk. "Angelo said you had a lady friend disappear?"

"Yes, she's one of my dancers and a close personal friend. I have a strip club, the Side Door lounge, and she worked for me. I don't want to involve the police if I can help it, I called Angelo for advice, he's actually my cousin, and he told me about you. I need someone to find her and make sure she's all right."

"If I agree to help you, I have to ask, why don't you want the police involved?"

He paused for a short time then said, "She's an illegal immigrant, I don't want her sent back to Russia and to certain death."

**

Chapter 2

"Okay, I'm intrigued, start from the top, you are?"

"My name is Ron Santos, I've owned the Side Door Lounge for about six years and we've never had any problems until recently. There's another strip club nearby, Heaven's Gate, that has recently changed owners and since then, they have been trying to hustle my dancers into working for them. Good dancers, who can work and shake it, are hard to find."

"So these new owners have been in your club. Have they made threats to you or your girls?" I asked.

"They come in occasionally and have made no serious threats yet, but I've heard from the girls that they are asking them to jump ship and work for them. They're a strange bunch, there's usually three of them and they are always dressed in black suits. I thought they were cops or Feds when they first appeared, they ordered soft drinks, so I figured they were working. Then one of my girls told me what they wanted. I just stayed away from them as long as they stayed cool. Then last week, one of my girls said that they told her she should come work for them or she may regret not making the move."

"What was the regret?"

"They didn't say, the girl just walked away from them and came to tell me, the men got up and left before I could approach them. They haven't been back since."

"Do you think they could have been behind the disappearance of your dancer, uh, what is her name?" I asked.

"I'm sorry, it's Marina Koska, she disappeared day before yesterday. Her roommate said she didn't come home after her shift at the club, and she hasn't been seen since. I don't know if they were behind it, they never really threatened harm, but maybe it's a warning."

"They could be saying quietly that this is what could happen if the girls don't cooperate. They don't have to announce that they did it, just makes people nervous." I offered.

"Yeah, my girls are all scared now, so I have to be extra careful. I hired a couple new bouncers to work the door and watch the girls."

"Do the girls leave alone or in groups at the end of their shifts?" I asked.

"I encourage them to leave in groups, strip clubs do attract a few strange people, never can tell who's a rapist or a serial killer." He made a face, like he wanted to strangle someone.

"Back in the early 70's I used to live in strip clubs, Duchess Lounge was my favorite." I said, he acknowledged the place, "I know what the men can be like in there. You said Marina is an illegal, she the only one in your club?"

He looked sheepish; his eyes went to the floor, generally a sign of avoidance. "I do have a few girls who have questionable credentials, look; I try to give them a start here until they can establish citizenship. I help them get away from the Russian Mafia in their country who force good looking women into prostitution and stripping in their clubs for little or no pay. The girls who refuse usually end up in a black body bag or at the bottom of the Volga. Marina ran away from that life and I gave her a chance. She's kind of special to me."

"How did you find these girls with questionable credentials to bring them here?" I asked.

"I have a friend who lives in Kiev and he has underworld connections there. I'd rather not say what kind, but it has to do with the government, ours I mean. He frequents many of the clubs looking for black market dealings and he has connections with a couple shipping companies where he has smuggled numerous women out in packing cases. It's not the best form of travel, but at least they reach their destination and hopefully freedom."

"The Russian Mafia there doesn't know he does this?"

"He'd be dead if they did, but Chaz is a lot crazy and not afraid of much. He hates injustice and he's a sneaky bastard. He could smuggle the body of Stalin out of the country if he put his mind to it."

I laughed to myself at the image of Stalin in a shipping crate. "Okay, Marina left work, heading home and never showed. How did she get home, car, cab or walk?"

"She didn't have a car; it would mean she'd need a driver's license, of course that would be impossible. She usually took a cab; they generally hang around the club at shift change for a fare. I asked the cabbies last night if any of them seen her or gave her a ride and they said they hadn't. She was pretty independent and usually went out by herself at night, when I wasn't around. Otherwise, I'd walk her to a cab. The night she vanished I wasn't around." He looked sad and rubbed his face with his massive hands.

I handed him my fee card and said I would help if he wanted me. He looked at the card and said money was no problem, he just wanted Marina back, safe and in one piece. I handed him my pad and pencil and asked him to write down any information about Marina that would help me to find her and some contact info to reach him. I asked if he had a picture of her, he said he'd get one to me.

"I need to ask, before I go getting myself in trouble, is this rival club mob connected?" I was concerned.

"Oh, hell, no. If it were, I'd be treading water carefully. I think there is some biker gang connection, but I'm not sure where the operational money comes from. At least I haven't heard that the club was mob connected and Angelo said he would check on it for me, quietly. I haven't heard anything yet."

"Another question, why don't you want Angelo's family connections involved?"

"The mob families here are not too friendly with the Traviano family, so having Angelo push would be a minor disaster. And I don't want to see anyone get whacked, as they say on TV." He smiled. "I let him

17

do some snooping to see what we were up against, that's all, and I don't want Angelo getting in trouble."

"Angelo is good at finding out things, if he finds out anything about the club; let me know right off, please. I don't want to go in bending over with my pants down."

Ron laughed at my reference, went to his back pocket, and took out his wallet attached to a heavy chain attached to his belt. Biker wallet. He opened it and took out five hundred in large bills and dropped it on my desk saying, "The advance, and let me know any progress you have."

"For Angelo's cousin, I'll keep you posted." I smiled, handed him my card and we stood, shook hands and he said, "I hope you will be very discreet about her being illegal, I want her to stay." I said I would and he left.

I picked up my phone and dialed Trapper, he came on by the second ring, "Richards, do you think I have nothing better to do than take calls from you?"

"Yes, I do believe you have nothing better to do." I smiled.

"Okay, I don't. So what do you want this time, information, background check, license plate ran, what?"

I had to hold in a laugh, "You like naked women, right?"

He was making heavy breathing noises now, "Yeah, whatcha got?"

"You ever heard of a strip club called Heaven's Gate?" I asked.

"Yeah, down around Seven Mile Road in Detroit. Why?"

"Know much about it?"

"No, but I'd be more than happy to check it out for you." Now I could see the wide grin on his face through the phone.

"Naked women and hookers, you would be in heaven. I have a case, no info right now, confidential, but it may involve the Heaven's Gate Lounge. I'd really appreciate anything you could get on it. They've had an ownership change in the last couple of months and I need to know who has it now. Before I blunder into something I don't want."

"You going in shooting. That sounds a bit dangerous for your old body to handle." He grinned again.

"Yeah, well if you have any connections with any Detroit cops who can help, it would be nice."

"Okay, so I'm a cop, why do you think I know everyone in law enforcement? I know a meter maid in Detroit, that's about it."

"Does the meter maid hook on the side?" I asked.

"No, but she puts out for free. So what is this mysterious case you have?" Trapper asked.

"Missing person. That's about all I can say till I gather some more intel."

"Intel, you on some sort of military operation?"

"Nope, just a simple case of finding a missing young lady, that's all I can say." I offered.

"Okay, play dumb, but if it comes down to anything dangerous, don't call me. I'll see what I can get on the strip joint for you, but you'll owe me."

"Don't I always, thanks and talk later." We hung up and I sat back in my chair, contemplating calling Buck. He was probably enjoying himself out in Sin City, but he might want to get in on the action of strip joint investigating. Besides, he doesn't need all that sex out there. It'll wear him out. I reached for the phone.

**

Chapter 3

"That's right, a strip club, I have a missing person to find, a young dancer who disappeared from the strip club. That's about all that's going on here." I didn't come right out and suggest he come back, I just told him how my work was doing here and let him make his own decisions. He was quiet for a moment, and then he said to hold on. He put his hand over the mouthpiece of the phone, but I could hear through his fingers.

"Maria, it's Jimmy, I can tell he's having problems with a really big case, I really think I should go back and bail him out... Yeah, he needs me, I can tell... I know, I'd miss you too, baby, but Jimmy is really in over his head on this one... Yeah, babe, I can come back after I help my friend solve his case. It shouldn't take too long... You got it." He came back on the phone and said, "Hey, can you pick me up at Metropolitan airport, I'll call with my flight arrival. You really need my help on this one, Jimmy. I'll talk later," and he hung up.

I hated myself, but I really could use the big guy to help me. This case sounded a bit dangerous, maybe. Buck loves danger and doesn't take crap from anyone. That's what I needed to go into the jaws of death and work this case. Okay, I'm being dramatical but he really would help right now. Besides Buck loved anything to do with strip bars, so this was right up his alley.

I didn't have anything more to do in my office, so I decided to close it up and head home. I couldn't see anything from Penny's show that I would have to worry about when I arrived. I closed up and drove out 15 Mile Road and down to our modest home on Lake St. Clair. I pulled into the drive, parked in my space, and went in to find Penny standing at the snack bar between the kitchen and the family room. She had a bunch of boxes on the counter and gave me a really big grin when I came in the front door. Willy was bouncing around my feet; I reached down and petted him.

"Sweetie, you're home, I'm so glad." I suddenly felt a chill when she said that. I came over to her as she threw her arms around me and gave me a big kiss. She backed off and said, "Take your shirt off, please." I was a bit taken back by that and asked why. She said just do it and started to unbutton my shirt. I knew it would do no good to fight her, so I let her strip me from the waist up.

She examined my arms and chest and picked up some kind of pad with a strap around the back of it. She slid it on her hand and proceeded to stroke the thing down my arm causing a raw burn as it ran across the hairs on my arm. I yelled in pain, and pulled my arm back and looked to where she had rubbed off the hairs.

"What the hell was that?" I demanded. She laughed and said it was a hair removal device that they show on TV, and she wanted to try it on a really tough load of hair. She knew I didn't like the hair on my body and once when we were a bit tipsy, all right a lot tipsy, she shaved my upper body of all the hair she could find, short of my beard and the sparse hair on my head. I was in pain from razor burn for days when I sobered up.

I looked at my arm and the hair was gone from the area she ran the thing down. I looked to the other boxes on the counter and asked, "Is that the only body torture device you brought home from your show?"

She took my arm again and started to finish the job, saying, "Yes, the rest are household miracle devices." She was a little more careful with the pad this time and made me sit on a stool while she finished my arm. I said that I was a bit unbalanced with one arm smooth and the other hairy. She worked on the other and it came out well. It didn't hurt as much as the razor incident and I was pleased with the results.

"So how was your day?" she asked.

Strip Club Murders

"I had a call from Angelo, our wiseguy from Vegas. He has a cousin in Detroit who needs a young lady found, she's missing."

"Angelo! How is he? Is Francis Traviano all right?" she said excitedly.

"Good and yes. Everyone is fine; Angelo just called for a favor. I have a case now to find a missing woman." I didn't really want to say more, but I didn't like keeping things from Penny, I usually regretted it. "Okay, you'll find out soon enough, the woman I'm supposed to find is a stripper at a club in Detroit. She went missing two days ago and her boss-slash-boyfriend is worried, so he called his cousin Angelo and Angelo recommended me."

"Why doesn't he just go to the police?" Penny asked as she played with a kitchen device from the pile.

"Well, that's the kicker; it seems the missing girl is not a citizen of the U.S. and would be deported back to Russia if the police were involved." I answered.

"Ah, I see. So when do we go to the strip club?" she asked with eyes wide. I knew this would happen, especially after the visit to the strip club out in Vegas.

"We is not the word right now. Sorry, but Buck is flying back tomorrow and he and I are going to check out the place to be sure it's safe then maybe you can come to get your jollies." I said as firm as I could.

"Okay, but I want to study the dancers so I can perfect my routine on our stripper pole, which we haven't shared much lately, why is that?"

"I honestly don't know, getting tired if it? Or is it just that we dive into sex without any stimulus beforehand. When a man goes to a strip club, he knows he won't get any sex from the woman there, so the excitement is the expectation to have great sex when he gets home to his wife. We just jump into it because we don't need the stimulus; you're horny all the time."

She whacked my arm and said to behave. "You think this club could be unsafe for me? And why is Buck coming back from his love nest with Maria?" She grilled me now.

"I talked to him today and he asked what I was up to and I told him. I didn't ask him to come back; it was his decision, he was anxious to do it."

"Especially when you mentioned a strip club, that was low. You knew he couldn't resist that. I'm ashamed to call you my husband." She smiled and aimed some kind of device at me and started poking me with it. I grabbed at it and examined the thing; it was some kind of device for scrapping the crud off your feet. I handed it back to her and told her to keep it away from me. She put it back on the counter and put her arms around me.

"Want to go watch me on the stripper pole?" she smiled.

"Only if you're naked." I grinned back. She let me go and started heading to the porch where the pole was mounted, I just stood there and then I saw her arm come around the door holding her blouse. I went to the porch.

A couple hours later, we were in our usual place on the couch, with our chips and beer watching TV. Willy was sound asleep on his chair I bought from the motel during the magic convention.

"You do a good job on the pole, I was stimulated." I said between munches on my chips.

"Well, I do take a quick spin every day while you're still at your office, just for the exercise." she said.

"Maybe I can install a pole at my office and you can come by to exercise there." I said hopefully.

"Never mind, I like my quiet time. That way I can dance to the song Lady by Styx and not get you all excited."

"That's mean." I pouted.

My cell phone rang and the caller ID said it was Trapper. I told Penny I was taking it in the kitchen, I answered and said "Whatcha got?"

"Well, I contacted a friend in the precinct that covers that part of town, name's Earl Daws, homicide Lieutenant, and he said the Heaven's Gate Lounge was purchased by a consortium out in New York. It's a company named Rex Erotica, Earl says it translates to "King Porn", and they own numerous strip clubs in New York City. They've been under investigation for trafficking in prostitution and possible slavery. Your missing girl could be in real trouble. Want the cops in on it; this could help to shut them down?"

"Will, you remember Angelo from Vegas?" I asked.

"Hell, yeah, great guy for a Mafia bone breaker." he laughed.

"Well, I'm working for his cousin here and the problem with the missing girl... I can trust you can't I?" He said I could, "Okay, the girl isn't exactly legal in this country, and to be found by the authorities would be cause for her to be sent back to her country of Russia and possible death." He was quiet as I waited for a reply.

"Well, then you've got your work cut out for you. Be careful and keep me informed."

**

Chapter 4

I was at Metropolitan Airport by 7 A.M. waiting for Buck's flight to arrive. I watched the people all milling about waiting for loved ones or friends to come in on the flights from places unknown. I saw a number of men, probably hired drivers, holding signs with people's names written on them, and thought it would be funny to make a sign saying "Obama" on it and stand by the waiting drivers. But I knew the airport security took a dim view of humor, so I just sat watching for Buck.

Around 7:45, Buck came down the hall with that big smile of his; I got up from my chair and went to him. He had only one carry-on bag and we left the concourse and out to parking.

"Did any investigating yet at the strip joint?" He asked first off.

"No, I was waiting for my partner to get back from his vacation so we could get down to business." I smiled.

"Well, it's time for business, talk to me, what's the story?" He asked.

I told him everything I knew from Ron and Trapper and that we needed to go to the Side Door Lounge first and start from there. He said that worked for him and that he was ready to go.

We drove up I-94 freeway from the airport and got off at Van Dyke Avenue then over to Seven Mile Road. I turned west and drove about two blocks to the club. It was just as I remembered from back in the seventies when I used to travel from club to club and this place was one of my stops. I parked on the side road and we walked to the door.

The tiny vestibule was still there and we went through the inner door. The club was dark of course, and the spotlights were flashing around the room. On stage in the middle side of the room, a young girl was gyrating to a Billy Ocean song, "Get outta my Dreams." She looked young enough to be my granddaughter, which made me very sad.

Ron was behind the bar, gave me a big smile, and waved. Buck and I went to the bar, I introduced Buck and they shook hands. Buck asked if Ron rode with a cycle club and Ron said he liked being independent. Buck agreed. Ron asked if we wanted a drink, I said too early for me and Buck said he'd have a diet Sprite. I said I'd take a Pepsi if they had it, he did. I told Ron that we'd talk in a bit; we just wanted to watch the show first. He smiled and said to enjoy ourselves.

We watched three dancers do their stuff and then I told Buck that we needed to start doing our job. I called to Ron and he told his other bartender to take over. He took us to his office in the back and we sat at his desk.

"Heard anything?" I asked.

"Not a goddamn thing. It's like she never existed." He made a face.

I told him about contacting a friend with the cops, I said he was cool with it, and told Ron what Trapper told me. He banged his fist on his desk and cursed.

"Buck and I are going to Heaven's Gate and check it out, have you been there recently?"

"No, not in a few years. I needed to see what the competition was doing and it's the same crap everywhere, stages and dancers. It's just the quality of the place and dancers that makes the difference. I run a clean establishment, good dancers and friendly environment, a place you could take your woman to."

I thought of Penny. "You've had no ransom demands or threats at all?"

"Nope, nothing, no words at all."

30

"Did you come up with a picture of Marina?" I asked.

"Yeah, I got one out of my photo book." He opened a drawer in his desk and took out a photo of him and Marina at some party. I thanked him and put the photo in my shirt pocket.

"Do you know anyone who works at the Gate?" I inquired.

"I knew one dancer, name of Brandy Wine, not her real name of course, but she may still be working there."

"Okay, I'll call if I need any more info." I nodded at Buck and we stood, everyone shaking hands and went out of the office. Buck stopped to smile at the girl on the stage then followed me out.

In my car I said, "Wow, I remember when I used to hang in these places, the girls were all in my age group, now I feel like I'm a pedophile watching these young things." Buck laughed out loud and said as long as they were over 21 he didn't care. I'm sure he didn't.

We drove over to Mound Road just south of Seven Mile Road and found Heaven's Gate, into the parking lot and I sat there, Buck waited.

Strip Club Murders

"I think we should go in separately, you go first and sit at a table by the bar, make sure there is a stool by your table and I'll come in and sit at that stool, watch my back." I said. I let Buck go first and then I waited about five minutes and went in.

I went into the rather large room that had two stages, one at each end of the room. I went to the long bar by the back and sat on a stool at the bar next to Buck's table. He had his diet Sprite already and was enjoying the dancer on the well-lit stage, but I could see he was watching me as well.

The bartender came up and asked me what I wanted to drink. I don't like drinking so early and not while I'm driving, but one draft wouldn't hurt. He went off to get my beer and then came back with it. I dropped a five and he went to get my change. When he came back, I asked if Brandy Wine still worked here, he gave me a strange look and said there was no girl by that name working. I thanked him and he went off.

About five minutes later two men in white shirts and narrow black ties came over. They were fairly ordinary looking, medium build, clean cut and kind of dumb looking, they reminded me of Jehovah's Witnesses on a Saturday morning. The one in front asked me why I wanted to know about Brandy Wine.

"I just wanted to know if she still worked here, a friend asked me to look her up. Why, is it a crime to ask?"

The front man just stared, then said, "She doesn't work here anymore so don't bother to ask. Understand?"

"Okay, do you know where she went; I'll go there and leave you guys alone." I said.

"I said don't ask anymore. Understand?"

"I'm very capable of understanding what I'm told; I just don't understand why I have to understand."

"Don't be a smart ass or you can leave right now." He started to reach for my arm just as Buck grabbed his and held it tightly in place. The man's arm was just suspended there, as he looked up to Buck who stood a whole head taller than he did. Buck was ready to grab the other man by his throat, but the man just backed away and watched from a short distance.

"Okay, I understand that you don't want to talk about Brandy. I'm just making small talk, but you seem to be a rather rude person." I stood and told Buck to let him loose, the man was rubbing his arm and backed away. I stepped towards him and asked, "Since you don't want to talk about Brandy, who can I talk to about her, or a girl named Marina Koska. Ring a bell?"

His eyes started darting past me and I turned with my hand in my jacket on my Glock, to find a woman coming towards Buck and me. She was attractive, svelte, wearing a tight black cocktail dress and done up in heavy make-up, a bit too much. I took my hand out of my jacket, but Buck kept his hand in his jacket, just in case.

"May I help you sir? What seems to be the problem?" Her voice was a bit gravely sounding like she had way too many cigarettes in her life.

I smiled and said, "I have no problem, but your boys do. I just asked if Brandy Wine still worked here, a friend asked me to look her up. That's no crime is it?"

"No crime to ask, we just had problems with Brandy, she was stealing from us and then ran off, and we like to know who is asking for her. We'd like to find her, and you are?"

"I'll tell you who I am, if you tell me who you are."

"I'm Elaina, manager of this bar. Now your turn."

"I'm a private investigator looking for a missing girl also, name's Marina Koska, sound familiar?"

"No, should it?"

"Well, it seems that three of your boys have been coming into the Side Door Lounge making subtle threats about his girls moving over to your club. Then about two days ago Marina disappeared, that something you'd know about?"

"I'm not even sure who these three men would be, I don't authorize my employees to solicit other dancers to come here. We have enough of our own girls to work with." She smiled demurely.

"Another question, do you come from around here, or did Rex Erotica bring you in from New York?"

Her smile faded and said, "Enjoy your drinks, watch the show, then I think you should leave." She turned and walked away quickly.

I think I hit a nerve.

**

Chapter 5

I sat back on the stool as the two boys went off to a table by the back and sat watching us. Buck was now sitting at the bar with me. "Thanks for the back-up. I was worried you might hurt them."

He smiled, "I held back my primal urges. Besides it would be a waste to kill such frail children."

Strip Club Murders

We watched the girls dance and I estimated that there were about ten of them around the room. They were busy giving lap dances and talking up the customers. They avoided us, probably by orders. I could see they were soliciting; I wasn't born in a manger. Buck asked if he could take a couple home, I said on his own time.

"It's weird that this club has such wimpy bouncers and thugs. Doesn't it seem strange to you?" I asked.

"I was just thinking that, if a bunch of my cycle buddies came in here, the help would probably wet their pants. Doesn't make sense." He replied. "You look at the Side Door, Ron has some real knuckle busters working the door, what do they have here, High School Musical."

"Yeah, strange." One dancer was walking by and I stopped her. She looked frightened and I asked if she knew Marina Koska, she said no and went off in a hurry after looking back at the boys still at their table, trying to look menacing.

"I don't think we're going to get any more help in here, maybe we came on a little too strong. Let's wait outside for shift change and have a talk with the girls." We drank up and as we went out, I waved to Heckle and Jeckle as they just sat stoney faced.

We sat in my car for about an hour, then around 4 P.M., the girls started to come pouring out, since their replacements had already went in. I didn't figure that this club would worry about the safety of its girls outside, so we hopefully could talk without interruption. As they came out, Buck and I got out of my Crown Vic and I asked out loud if anyone was brave enough to talk to us? Three of the girls stopped as the rest just went off and then they came over.

"I need some information; any of you fine ladies want to talk?" I asked as I flashed a twenty-dollar bill, one girl came up a bit too close and I asked her nicely to step back, she did reluctantly. I said she could do that to Buck; she did and took the twenty. He smiled and I asked in her ear if she knew a Marina Koska? She looked over to me, as she rubbed up to Buck and stroked his shoulders, he was enjoying the ride, then she said she'd talk if we met her away from this place. I asked where, she said at a Ram's Horn Restaurant on Van Dyke above Eight Mile. I said we could do that and she went off with the two other girls. Buck was resting against my car and I had to smack him, then he came to. We got into the car and drove over to the restaurant.

The girls were already in a large booth and had menus. I was feeling this was going to be expensive. They all slid around as Buck and I came up, I let Buck slide in next to the girls and I sat next to him. One girl on the other side of the booth pouted and asked why I didn't want to sit next to her. I said I was married to a woman who carries a large gun, I feared for my life.

Strip Club Murders

They introduced themselves, Tiffy, Buffy and Rose. I knew those weren't their real names but I didn't fuss about it.

The waitress came up and we ordered, then she went off.

"Okay, you said you may have some info for us?" I asked the girl, Tiffy, who turned Buck on by the car.

"Are you the cops?" Was the first thing she asked.

"I'm a private investigator, looking for a missing girl; it could have been anyone of you." I said as I looked around the table.

They all were quiet, then Tiffy spoke again, "Anything we say is going to be private, right?" I agreed. "I've worked at Heaven's Gate for going on three years. It was a good club, but since these new owners took over, things have slowly changed."

"How so?" I asked.

"There have been more girls working now, cutting into my tips. The new manager, Elaina, has been pushing us to be friendlier to the customers, if you know what I mean. I don't like it." The other girls were agreeing with her. "I work hard dancing and I earn my tips but I draw a line at hooking. I got a daughter to raise and I couldn't look at her honestly, if I was putting out sexually. Dancing and teasing for tips is one thing, hooking is another."

Another girl, Buffy, spoke up, "They have also been telling us to recruit new girls to work in their clubs in New York, too. I've brought in a few, but they went off to New York and I haven't heard from any of them since."

I asked, "Have any of you ever heard of a girl named Marina Koska?"

Rose said she knew Marina from when she worked at the Side Door six months ago. I asked, "Why did you leave the Side Door?" She said for more money, "Heaven's Gate is a bigger club and had more customers, but since the new owners are bringing in more girls, I haven't made the same cash." I asked if she knew where Marina might be now, she said she didn't. I showed the picture Ron gave me of Marina to the other two girls and they said they didn't recognize her.

"How many new people working the club now, I mean managers, bouncers, bartenders, who came in after the change of ownership?"

Tiffy offered, "There's only Elaina managing, then they brought in eight pasty boys, I call them that, as bouncers... "She laughed, "They couldn't bounce a baby on their knee if they tried. The bartenders are the same as before, but they did bring in two new ones. That's about it. Occasionally three rather large bruisers come in and they go off to Elaina's office, we don't know what that's about, but the men aren't one's I'd mess with." She looked up to Buck, "They were kinda like you." She smiled.

"I'm a pussycat, I do no harm. Unless I get pissed off." Buck grinned.

"Have there been any unusual rumors about the new owners?" I asked.

Tiffy said, "I've heard they're some kind of company that has dealings with foreign places besides New York, I once heard Elaina speaking on the phone some kind of language I didn't know. They haven't been with us long enough to really get a feel for them. She has mentioned to us frequently about going to New York to work at their clubs there, but I said I had family here and wasn't interested in moving."

Buffy spoke, "There have been a few girls that we were told suddenly went off to New York, but they never said they were going, they just disappeared and Elaina said they did go to New York."

Buck looked at me and quietly said, "Think there's a trip to New York in our future?"

"Too early to tell but we may need to take a quick trip later." I replied.

Our food arrived and we ate while talking about the business of stripping. I was relating my experiences in the past of my travels around the club circuit and the girls I had met along the way. We finished and I paid, of course.

The girls all went off while Buck and I stood by my car. "I don't know, but the people working this place are all a bit odd for a strip club. Their bouncers are ridiculously powerless if real trouble broke out. Unless they're secretly Ninjas, I would imagine them running the other way from trouble. Elaina seems too much a refined woman for this type of work, compared to Ron; he fits in a strip club. Although she reminds me of a madam, the fancy prostitute kind."

"And there's the connection, this all boils down to prostitution." Buck grumbled.

"Trapper mentioned that there may be some slavery trafficking involved, Tiffy said that she thought there were foreign dealings, that's generally where women are sold out for slavery. I'm hoping Marina isn't in on that, if so she's probably out of the country by now." I said sadly.

It was now just about 5:30 P.M. and I hadn't seen Penny's show today, so I had no idea of what to expect when I got home. That had me a bit worried, but I would suck it up and take it like a man. I walked around the car to the driver's door and said, "Let's take one more trip to the Side Door and let Ron know what we found. I hope he takes it well."

**

Chapter 6

Ron just sat quietly, not moving. I was a bit concerned, he wasn't responding to my report on the status of his girl.

"Are you all right on this, you don't seem to be upset?" I asked. Buck was sitting next to me; he was being quiet as I talked.

"I'm very upset, but I know it doesn't do much good to scream and yell. Maybe a little outburst occasionally, but I have very high blood pressure and I've been warned that it's not good for me to get too excited. So I will take my frustrations out on a punching bag later on." He spoke quietly and calmly.

He smiled, but I knew he was holding his rage in.

"Are you giving up?" he asked.

"Oh, hell, no. We've just begun, I intend to find Marina or put away the people who may have caused harm to her. I mean that."

"Thank you, I'm depending on you two to find her."

"We will, count on it." Buck spoke this time. He thanked us and Buck and I left. I dropped Buck off to his house, I drove home, and as I rode quietly along Jefferson Avenue, I thought about the day. It had been long and not really profitable in the sense of information, but we had a start.

I pulled into the drive and parked. As I went into the house, I could smell incense and the lights were down low. I came in and announced my arrival just as music blared out from somewhere in the kitchen. It was Middle Eastern music and then Penny came out from the kitchen in a belly dancing outfit, complete with a veil over her face. She danced around me and bumped hips numerous times as she tried to do the dance correctly, but she needed practice. I wasn't going to tell her that, she was doing well enough for the effort.

The music was short and ended as she finished facing me. I raised the veil across her face and kissed her hard on the lips. She bumped bellies with me and asked if the Sheik would like to go into the tent for a little roll in the sand.

"I presume you had a belly dancer on your show today?" I asked.

She nodded enthusiastically and said, "Madam Katrinka, fortune teller and belly dance teacher, she gave a couple readings and then she taught my audience and myself a few good belly dancing moves. The kind that I think would work well in bed also."

I said to show me, and she did.

About two hours later, after we belly danced in bed and took a short nap, we were in our usual spot in front of the TV. I asked Penny if Madam Kinky read her fortune.

"That's Madam Katrinka, not Kinky." She laughed.

"Oh, right, you are Madam Kinky."

"Okay, Kinky maybe, any way's, she read my cards and said I was in for good fortune, and a happy life," she smiled.

"I'll bet she says that to all the gullible people." I replied.

"I'm not gullible, I don't believe a word she said, although I did like the good fortune part she mentioned."

"You didn't believe the happy life part? You mean you're not happy with me?" I asked.

"I married you, didn't I?"

"You didn't answer the question."

"I like sex with you, don't I?"

"Still avoiding the question."

"Sweetie, I am so happy with you it hurts."

"Okay, I'll take that as an answer."

"So, have you found your missing stripper yet, and when can I go to the strip club?" She poked me in the ribs and smiled.

"No and soon." I smiled back. "Buck and I did a little scouting around the rival club and it's a bit strange there."

"Strange?"

"Yeah, it's like a boy scout camp with naked counselors." I explained what Buck and I found at the club and what we found out at our lunch with the girls.

"Were the girls naked at lunch?" She poked me in the ribs again.

45

"Not totally, there was a dress code for the restaurant, we all had to wear ties, and clothes were optional."

"So, what are you going to do next?"

"Well, I think I need to find out more about Rex Erotica. That's the key to the whole thing."

"And have you Googled it yet?" she asked.

"No, I was going to when I got home, but I got distracted." I smiled.

"You have to stop letting things distract you." She grinned.

"I wish I could." I sighed and kissed her on the nose.

A short time later, Penny was watching some show about a woman in a hospital with some odd ailment and the doctors were arguing about how to treat her. I worried about our health care providers when they couldn't agree.

I was pouring over the internet hunting down Rex Erotica, and finding more than I thought I would. The first place I visited was their "official" website and it was basically a glossy, high-energy showboat of their holdings around the world. They had what they referred to as exotic dance clubs where the women excite your every dreams. A listing of clubs said they had about ten clubs in New York, six around Hong Kong, three in California and one so far in Detroit, but they say there will be more here. I wondered if the city of Detroit knew about this, or the other club owners.

I did a search on WhoIs.com, the place to find out who owns a web address, for the web address of RexErotica.com and it came up to a webhosting company in New York City. I copied off the page for future reference.

I found a forum that some guy started a thread about their clubs in New York. He was complaining that he was robbed by one of the girls and the manager of the club treated him rudely when he complained to them. He said the girl gave him a lap dance and took his money off the table while he was distracted. There was one other posting on the forum from a man who claim a dancer solicited him and he paid heavily for a blowjob, and when he objected to the price, some big goon came up and threatened him. I thought that the boys at the Heaven's Gate would probably do the blowjob there instead of the girls.

I did find one small post on another website that was warning women to stay away from Rex Erotica clubs; she said they were into slave trafficking. The person who submitted the post was a woman who said she escaped from one of their slave clubs and barely survived the ordeal. The police investigated the allegations, but came up with nothing. The girl accused the Vice officers who checked her allegations of being in on it. That wasn't good. The girl had an email address and I copied it down, for future reference.

I checked a couple of other websites that mentioned the clubs, mostly good, some bad. The bad posts were mostly about the treatment they received while at the clubs, from both the girls and the bouncers. I found that forums generally had many people who liked to bitch just because they want to be heard, even if they were wrong.

I finally found one website that was what I would call a corporate website, it detailed the objective of the company, corporate headquarter locations and their officers. I thought this was a bold thing to do if you are a crime organization. I did a page copy so I could print it out later, and didn't find anything more on Rex Erotica.

I opened up my mail program and typed a brief email to the woman who wrote about her ordeal with the slave aspect of it. Her email address was Lana579@gmail.com and I wanted to word it carefully.

"Lana579, I'm a private investigator in the Detroit, Michigan area and saw your posting on the forum about Rex Erotica. I have a case involving a missing woman that may have something to do with a local club here owned by Rex Erotica. I'd like to talk to you about your experience and maybe it will help both me and you to stop these people. My email address is privateeye1@mail.com, or my phone number is 586-555-3680, please contact me, Jim."

I hit the send button and off it went; I hoped she still was on the other end.

I checked my email and read a couple of RSS feeds with the news of the day, seemed a couple more celebrity couples were divorcing, why do they bother to get married in the first place, they never make it. I checked my email again, nothing, and then closed up the computer.

I looked at my can of beer on the computer desk, it was still the beer I've drank forever, Milwaukee's Special Reserve light, which most of my friends called piss beer, but I grew fond of it and it was the cheapest beer I could buy for a 30 pack back when I was poor. Sure, I had the money now to buy the better stuff, but why, when this stuff was just as good. And it didn't give me a headache in the morning.

I went back over to Penny who was into her sixth tissue from my count on the table. She sniffled and looked to me with red eyes and said the woman was going to make it. I looked to the TV and smiled.

* *

Chapter 7

Around 9 P.M., my cell phone rang and it was Trapper. I answered and said I was off duty.

"Do I care; you are on duty 24/7 now that you are a public servant. All law enforcement is expected to be on duty. Okay, talk to me about Rex Erotica."

I was a bit surprised by his curt question. I guess he was concerned about my case. I told him what Buck and I went through today between Ron and Heaven's Gate. He listened quietly and then he asked if I knew what Marina looked like. I said that Ron had given me a photo when we were in his office earlier and I described her.

"Good, the girl wasn't her. I was called earlier by Earl Daws and he said they found the body of a girl that turned out to work as a stripper at the Gate. He asked about my inquiry of the Gate since he was trying to put his case together, he asked why I wanted to know and I told him. I didn't say anything about your girl's residency, just that she was missing and you were looking for her. Jim, the Detroit police are looking to close down the Heaven's Gate operation and I would recommend being careful hanging around the place."

"Thanks for the heads up. Do you think I could talk to your friend Daws, would he be cooperative?" I asked.

"Earl is a crazy guy, he loves a mystery and I think you two would get along nicely. But I didn't say that." He laughed and hung up.

I sat there for a minute and thought about what to do now. I was tired and I was wearing down, old age creeping in. I looked to Penny and asked if she was ready for bed.

"Damn, you're just a sexual dynamo aren't you?" she looked with me a smile.

"No, I want to go to bed and sleep, we had enough sex earlier and I have a lot of things to do tomorrow." I said.

She gave me a pout and then sighed, "Okay, Sweetie. I am a bit worn out too."

We cuddled in bed and I finally slept, dreaming about kidnapping and murder. I woke about every hour during the night, and then woke around 6 A.M. but couldn't get back to sleep. I laid there thinking about the case and where I was going to go with it. I thought I was smart when it came to being a P.I., but

Strip Club Murders

I was feeling a little mortal now trying to work out a plan to find one woman who may be either dead, or in a slave ring in some foreign country.

I got up around 7:30 and started to get ready for my day. Penny was up shortly after, she was always bubbly in the morning, I hated that.

I called Buck and told him to be ready to start the day, I would talk about new info when I met him at my office; he said he'd be there. Penny went off with Willy to work and I finished my toast, then gathered my toys and went out the door to my office.

Buck was, of course, in his usual position on the lobby chair and he looked at me coming down the hallway, smiling. I got up to him and just kicked his feet because it was the thing to do. He grinned at me and got up to follow me into the office.

He went to the client's chair and I went to the answering machine, it was blinking. I pushed the button and there was one message, it was Ron, calling to ask me to call him. I went to my desk, picked up the phone, and called him.

"Jim, I heard on the news this morning that they found the body of a woman who was a stripper, was it Marina?" he sounded in a panic.

"Ron, calm down, it wasn't her. I had a call from my cop friend and he told me it wasn't her. We still have options to check so please take a breath and relax. I'll keep you informed with what we find and ignore the TV news, stop watching it."

He agreed and hung up. I looked to Buck and told him the new information I had from after we split yesterday. I told him about the stuff I got off the web and what Trapper told me.

My cell phone rang and I looked at the number that came up on the caller ID, it was from a New York area code. I answered and the voice on the other end sounded very young.

"Is this Jim?" The childlike voice asked.

"Yes, it is, who's calling?"

"My name is Lana; I posted online about the Rex Erotica. You sent me a message," she said.

"Ah, yes, I did. I'm glad you responded. I need to talk to you about your ordeal about the slavery. But let me explain why I'm looking into Rex Erotica. I was hired here in Michigan to find a missing girl who may have been taken by a Rex Erotica club in Detroit, and I'm at a loss for information about the company or what they are up to. If you can tell me anything, it may help."

She was quiet for a bit then said, "I worked at one of their clubs in New York and after a while they kept badgering me to work for them in Hong Kong. I said I didn't want to go out of the country, and they stopped asking me. I figured it was over, but one day I was grabbed in the dressing room and taken to a place somewhere in the city. I was held with about six other girls and then one morning about two days later, we were being taken out to a waiting van. The person who was taking me was distracted by a loud noise, probably from a car backfire, and turned to see where it came from. I saw my opportunity and ran around the corner of the building and luckily, I ran out into the street just as a cop car was cruising by. They stopped when they saw a woman with hands tied and questioned me. I told them what happened but when they went to the alley to check, the van was gone. They accused me of being a hooker whose trick got out of hand. I was eventually taken to the strip club but the manager there told the cops I never worked there. The other girls were threatened not to say I worked there. The whole thing just went sour and I just got away from it all and just tried to forget about it. I was pissed, but what could I do." She finished.

"I'm sorry about your ordeal; do you know where they were going to take you that day?"

"I did hear something about planes and Hong Kong. I figured they were going to force me to work in their Hong Kong club whether I wanted to or not. The other girls with me had talked while we were being held, about slavery for men from the Middle East, I

54

didn't believe it but they could have been right. I'll never know, and I moved out of New York City to get away from them. I'm not saying where I am now; I don't really even know you to say."

"I understand, I wouldn't trust me either, if I didn't know me." She gave a quick laugh and I continued. "I'm going to keep at this till I find out what happened to my missing girl, if along the way I need you to talk to the police here, would you be agreeable to that?"

"If it would do any good, the police in New York blew me off, so what's to say yours won't."

"Because they are already investigating Rex Erotica here, and we have a murder of one of their girls that will need to be resolved, one way or another. Can I count on you to provide information?"

"Sure, what the hell, if it help, I'll do it. You have my email address and probably my phone number off your caller ID. So let me know, I'd like to see the bastards fry."

"Thanks, I'll be in touch." We said our good-byes and I hung up.

I took out the phone book and got the number for the Detroit Police and called them asking for Homicide Detective Earl Daws. They gave me his local number and I called it. After about four rings a man answered saying it was he.

"Detective Daws, I'm a friend of Will Trapper." He said he was sorry to hear that, I laughed, "I'm a private investigator and I have a case to find a missing girl, she worked at the Side Door lounge and the connection to her disappearance may be with the Heaven's Gate Lounge."

He was quiet for a bit then he said that Will already warned him about me, that I would probably pester the hell out of him, that was nice of Trapper, then he asked if I had anything that he may need to know. I told him briefly all that I had come by in the past couple days, everything except the fact that Marina was an illegal alien. He asked if I could come in to have a heart to heart about the case, I said I would and when I'd be there and we hung up.

I looked to Buck and asked if he wanted to go visit the Detroit police, he wrinkled up his nose and said he'd wait in the car.

**

Chapter 8

We drove down Van Dyke Avenue and as we passed into Detroit, at Eight Mile Road, I saw the Duchess Lounge on the right. Memories came flooding back to my days in the 70's going in to watch the girls dance and one in particular, Pixie. I still remember the veil dance she did to 'Lady' by Styx, which is now an inside joke between Penny and I. Then I thought maybe Buck and I could stop in later and see if the place has changed at all. I was sure Pixie wouldn't be working there now; she'd be in her late fifties or maybe even sixties now, probably not a pretty sight. I'd prefer to remember her as she was.

We arrived at the Six Mile area police precinct and I smiled and told Buck not to cause any trouble in the parking lot. I went in and asked the desk officer for Daws. He got on the phone and shortly after a tall, older man in a well-tailored suit came out and introduced himself as Daws. We went back to his office and shook hands after he said to call him Earl, and I said I was Jim. We sat.

"Will tells me you're a cracker jack P.I. and have taken down some really bad-ass killers. I remember the case of the two wackos who were murdering the cheerleaders. You did good on that." He said enthusiastically. "Will told me about the Dominatrix and Mistress killers, and then out in Vegas, how you guys brought down the Bridezilla killer. You're a one-man crime solving machine."

"I had help on all those; don't let my charm and my eye-for-crime fool you. There was a lot of good back-up work by the police and my associates to take down those killers, Will included. Now that we are done patting me on the back, let's talk Rex Erotica."

"We both have a case that seems to be connected and I don't want anything mucking up my case, I'm sure you'll keep me informed as to anything you may have on your mind to do, just so we're not shooting each other in the cross fire." He grinned.

"I am nothing if not cooperative, and I'll hold my fire till I see if it's you." I laughed.

"Okay, let's get our stories together so we can get it on track." He sat back and said, "Your story first."

"Before I start, there is one delicate matter that I need to cover if I'm going to share with you. Can I get some kind of guarantee from you that what I tell you about my case is strictly between us?"

"Is it anything illegal?" He asked.

"Well, it borders on not so legal, how do you stand on aliens?"

"Little green men or the type that cross our borders for the American dream?" He smiled.

"Border crossing type."

"Mexican?"

"Russian, female type."

"Mail order or smuggled."

"Smuggled in, by an agent of our own government."

"Hmm... Well if the government is behind it, I'm okay with it. Talk."

"Marina Koska escaped from the Russian mob and prostitution, by way of a packing case over the ocean to hopefully freedom. Ron Santos owns the Side Door, helped her get work, and get ready for the citizen swear-in. A couple weeks ago, three mild mannered gentlemen came in Ron's club and started to try to talk his girls into shifting employment over to Heaven's Gate. There was some opposition from the girls and then two days ago Marina turned up missing. Could be a subtle warning or they thought she was worthy of sending her back overseas into slavery. My partner and I talked to three young ladies about the club and they told us the same story, prostitution and slavery, both here and in Hong Kong."

I took a breath and Earl asked if I wanted something to drink, I said that would be nice. He went to a cube fridge in his office and opened it, asking if I liked Pepsi. I said is there any other soft drink. He handed me a can and I popped the top.

"As I said, my partner and I are trying to track Marina for Ron, he has a big crush on her and I'd hate to see him get mad if the Heaven's Gate club has her."

"I know Ron, I had occasion to talk to him over a murder that occurred near his club last year. He is big. I also presume he can be mean. But he was cooperative and concerned about his girls in light of murder nearby."

"He also has connections to a mob family in Mississippi; they were displaced from New York by the Feds a number of years ago, but still have clout in New York after Francis Mangelo, from Mississippi, married the New York Traviano family capo a couple months back in Vegas. That's where I met Ron's cousin, Angelo, a family enforcer, who recommended me to Ron."

"Why didn't the family get involved with the disappearance of Marina?"

"Ron wanted to keep this low-key, not an all-out mob war, if Rex Erotica is mob connected."

"I knew he was a smart man. I don't want to have to mop up dead bodies either. Okay, I'm cool with your missing girl, I really hope you find her; I'll help the best I can. Now my story, last night we got a call about a dead girl in the alley of a row of stores along Ryan Road below Seven Mile. The girl was in the system, dancers have to be registered to work, so we had her picture and prints. She worked at the Heaven's Gate. I sent a couple of plain clothes there with her crime scene picture and they reported that the slinky female manager said she had quit a few days before, wasn't happy with the new owners and their policies. She knew nothing more about the girl after she quit the club. One of the officers called the manager the ice queen. You met her, what's your opinion?"

"Well, she did seem to have a pole up her ass, not someone I'd take on a date." I offered.

"Yeah, about what the officer said. Anyway, our dancer was killed about the same time your girl went missing, think there's a connection?"

"Not sure, I still don't know why she was taken or possibly murdered for that matter. There's been no ransom demands or warnings to Ron's girls; she just vanished. I'm kind of hoping she just took off to avoid the hassles coming from the other club, possibly exposing her as an undocumented alien. Then again, I think she would have contacted Ron for all he's done for her. I'm baffled right now, not enough to go on."

"Welcome to my world. My vic was killed execution style, bullet to the back of the head from above, like she was on her knees when shot. Hands tied behind her and dumped where she was killed. No evidence from the kill, CSI found nothing in the alley but a mess of people going through it. We got nothing right now, just a dead dancer." He went quiet for a moment; I had nothing to say either.

"Well, as Trapper said, we got our work cut out for us." I asked if he needed me further and he said he didn't but to keep in touch. He gave me a couple of his cards, I gave him mine, and he said thanks. I left and back to Buck who was napping with his seat all the way back. I felt like kicking his feet but I couldn't reach them so just shook the car, until he jumped up. He grinned and hit the door lock and I got in.

"Glad to see you were on duty, nothing stolen from the lot while you're here, eh?" I laughed and started the car and headed out to the Side Door. I told Buck the story on the way and then we arrived and went in.

Ron was seated on a stool and jumped up to greet us. I didn't smile, I told him we had nothing yet and asked to go to his office.

"I hope you understand that we will do what we can to find her, but it may take time. This is not the movies where everything is solved in a couple hours." I said to get him to understand that concept.

"Hey, Jim I trust you to do what you can, I'll be patient." He said with a sad face.

I told him about the murder of the dancer from Heaven's Gate and that I had Detective Earl Daws on my side now. Ron said he remembered the detective from last year and said he was fair.

My cell phone rang and it was Daws again. I answered and he asked if I could come identify the body of a woman just found in a dumpster behind an unoccupied office building. Daws said he thinks it could be my missing girl. I asked if I could bring Ron, he said it would help to identify her. God, I hated to tell Ron.

**

Chapter 9

I told Ron what Daws had said and down played that it could be Marina, but Daws wanted positive ID that it was or wasn't. The three of us went to my car and drove over to the unoccupied building that Daws said they were at. We parked and walked up to the crime scene yellow tape and were stopped by a uniform. Daws saw us and yelled to let us through. He said to watch where we were walking around the little markers of evidence being photographed. I saw a couple of large caliber shells by the markers and the body was covered. The alley way was fairly secluded and it was just off the freeway so it was noisy, any gunfire would hardly be heard.

"Okay, this is not pretty, her face is about blown away by the gun fire and both hands were removed, definitely a hit. Ron, I'm sorry if this is your missing girl, but do you know anything about her that we can identify her without prints and facial?"

Ron stood looking at the body covered by the white sheet, then looked to Daws and said, "Yeah, she had a tiny butterfly tat on her left buttocks. She wanted me to get one, I said I'd be damned if I had a butterfly anywhere on my body. If it's there, then it's her." He choked a bit then turned away as the CSI officer went to the sheet and lifted it, examining the girl. He put the sheet down, came to Daws, and said there are no tattoos anywhere on her posterior. Ron heard that and gave out a choking breath of air and I saw the man weep, for joy I presume.

He walked away followed by Buck; I stood looking at Daws and said, "We got a small crime wave going on here. Think this girl could be a dancer too?"

"Can't tell right now, but she has a good body, well-toned like a dancer, could be. I'm getting to really dislike Heaven's Gate. Feel like taking a ride with me?" I said I would and told him I just had to get Buck to take Ron back in my car. I went and told Buck to drive Ron back and hang out at Side Door until I got there. He loved that idea and they went off after I gave him the keys.

Daws and I went to his clean looking, unmarked, 2009 Crown Vic police interceptor, I said I'd trade him my twenty-year-old Crown Vic, he laughed and then we drove over to Heaven's Gate.

We were stopped at the door by Heckle and Jeckle, still in their Sunday best outfits. Daws stared down Heckle as the little wimp stood in the way. Daws pulled his badge and said to move or be moved. Heckle looked towards the bar. Elaina was sitting on a stool by the corner with two rather large men. She saw us and stood to come over.

Strip Club Murders

"Gentlemen, can I help you?"

Daws pushed his arm into Heckle, shoved him aside, and came to the Ice Queen. "I'm Detective Lieutenant Earl Daws and I want you to look at my face and remember it. If I find out that two girls from your club where murdered, I may have all kinds of inspectors crawling around your establishment looking for any kinds of violations that can get you closed down until I solve my case. You have any other girls that recently quit, we got another body today, haven't ID'd her yet but we will. And I'll just bet she worked for you." He stood glaring into her face, she didn't twitch a muscle.

"Threaten all you want Detective, I have nothing to hide. If you are not here to drink, then obey the sign on the door that says we have the right to refuse entrance to anyone. Police or no. So unless you have a warrant, you can leave." She stood her ground. Daws just wanted to shake her up a bit, he told me that in the car coming over. He turned and looked at Heckle and Jeckle and laughed. Then he made a gun out of his hand and fingers and went bang to them. He turned to me and we left.

"Yeah, that went well." He said. "I had to get it out of my system and see what reaction I could get out of the bitch."

"Yeah, I loved how she ran in terror from your threats."

"Will said you could be a wise-ass." He smiled. "I got the reaction I wanted from her. Now that I have her attention, when I come in the next time, she'll be more receptive."

"You live in a different world, don't you?"

"Planet Nespo, I'm the supreme leader." He laughed.

We arrived at the Side Door and went in. Buck was camped out at a table surrounded by nubile semi-naked women, and looking like a king. He saw me and grinned.

Ron came over, shook Earl's hand, thanked him for his discretion about the body today, and asked if he wanted a drink. Earl said he was on duty, but if Ron could put a draft beer in a plastic cup, it would work for him. Ron asked me and I said I'd take a draft too. He went off and then brought our drinks to the table we took over from Buck. The women had all went back to work and we sat taking in the music and the naked ladies.

"I have to bring Penny back here or she's going to drive me nuts." I looked to Ron, as we all sat at the table, and asked, "Can you let my wife dance when we come in, she has a stripper pole at home she practices on."

Strip Club Murders

Buck looked to Ron and said, "His wife is Penny Wickens, the TV talk show woman, may be good for your business if she danced."

Earl looked at me, "You are really married to Penny Wickens, I thought Will was kidding when he said that. I knew she was involved in the cheerleader killings but I didn't know you were nailing her."

"Don't ever say I was nailing her in front of her. She'll rip you a new ass if she heard that." I laughed.

It's amazing, I can drink a six-pack of beer at home and not feel a thing, but one beer in a club and I get a little tipsy. I could never figure that out.

"Yep, we got married out in Vegas almost three months ago, after living together for about a year. I had to make an honest woman out of her." I smiled.

Ron was looking sad now, probably thinking of Marina. I looked at Earl and asked, "Do you think that Heaven's Gate may have some incriminating evidence in Elaina's office?"

"If you're going to do something illegal like breaking and entering, I don't want to know. But the club closes at 2 A.M. and is empty by 3:30. There is an alarm system that has a phone connection to the security service, but if the phone line, which is attached to the back of the building, were disabled, they wouldn't know. I didn't say any of this, I don't even know you." he smirked.

"How do you know about the alarms?" I asked.

"We used to get false alarms from them occasionally; we have to know how they have it set-up."

I looked at Buck and he smiled. I said we should call it a day and go get some sleep; we were going to have a late night. I winked at Earl and then said to Ron we were still with him. Buck and I got up and I looked at Earl, "You hanging around here?"

"Yeah, it's my civic duty to protect these fine female citizens of our great city." He smiled at me, "Be careful, I'd hate to have to tell Penny Wickens that her husband was shot as a burglar."

"I'm too good to get caught; besides Buck here is an expert on B and E." Buck protested that he was not. I took his arm and led him out.

We got in the car and I looked at my watch, it was just before 4 P.M. and I was still having to face Penny's surprises when I got home.

"I'll call you later and we can meet to go to the bar. Dress dark, I don't want to be seen."

"You're talking to a master criminal here; I have lots of dark clothes."

I swung by my office, dropped him to his car, and headed home. Penny wasn't visible when I went in, I feared for my life that she would come popping out and attack me. I yelled to her, but no answer and it was too quiet. Willy was also missing, now I was worrying a bit. I went out to the porch and it was empty, she wasn't on the pole. I went to our bedroom and saw a lump under the covers and Willy was zoned out on his chair. I went to the bed, pulled the covers back a bit, and saw my baby sleeping peacefully. I sat and stroked her hair, and then she came to and smiled at me.

"Welcome home, Sweetie." she said happily.

**

Chapter 10

"What are you doing in bed so early?"

"I was tired, and I'm not feeling so hot. I hope I'm not coming down with something. I figured bed rest would be good for me."

I felt her forehead and she was a bit warm. I told her to just rest and I'd make up some chicken soup for her. She thanked me and I went to the kitchen. I rummaged around in the cupboards looking through the cans of soup for chicken and finally found one. I ran the can through the opener on the wall and dumped it in a pan that was on the stove. I cooked it, poured it in a bowl, pulled out the small snack tray for the bed, and took it along with a glass of milk to her. She was propped up on the bed and I put the tray over her. She wasn't looking too good, eyes a bit droopy. I ruffled Willy who was now watching us from his chair and he jumped up on the bed using the pet stairs we bought so the tiny dog could join us.

"I hate to see you this way, but you should just rest tonight. Which is good because Buck and I are going to be doing some late night skulking." I said.

"Are you going out to get in trouble?" she looked up to me between slurps of soup.

"I hope not, there have been two murdered dancers now and I still have no leads to my missing girl. I have the unofficial blessings of the Detroit police to take a midnight rummage through Heaven's Gate." I got up, went to my side of the large closet, and pulled out some dark clothes.

"You're a cat burglar now?" She slurped the soup.

"Doing a reconnaissance mission. Something is hinky in Heaven and Buck and I are going to snoop."

"Won't God object?" She slurped again.

"I think whatever gods are watching over me, they would approve. I just wish I could get some divine intervention to help me find Marina. I'm hoping that we may find some information to lead us to an answer."

"Well, be careful, your warranty has expired and I can't afford to fix you." She slurped.

"What do you mean can't afford it, you make a good salary on your show, especially since it went national. Most people could live for a year on what you make in a month."

"I'm putting every dollar away for my retirement, I plan for the future. You just give your wealth away, you're too soft-hearted and that's why you'll never be rich." Big slurp.

"I won't be able to take it with me, which means you'll get what's left, so I give a little away to people who need it now. I'm generous."

She stopped slurping and looked to me, "Yes, Sweetie, you are a good person, I'll probably keep you." She went back to slurping.

I took her tray when she finished and tucked her in and said to just sleep, I didn't kiss her lips, not sure if she was coming down with something, so nipped her forehead, it was still warm. I turned out the room lights and went out to the kitchen again to make something to eat for myself. Willy had joined me, probably hadn't eaten either, I put food into his bowl and he attacked it without prompting.

I sat on the couch with Willy, watching the TV and eating my warmed up pizza rolls with store bought potato salad and then my phone rang. It was Earl.

"Hello supreme being of planet Nepso, what's up?"

"The coroner finished with the vic from today, he managed to get a serial number off her breast implants and got the info from some medical database. We got a name and checked the stripper database, the girl wasn't an employee of the Heavens' Gate, but she was an employee of the Red Door Lounge down off of Connor Avenue. I think that's interesting. I sent a couple of my men to the bar and they said the girl was missing from two days ago. Sound familiar?"

"Someone is hitting the clubs around the city, one girl from each maybe. Are they sampling the girl pool or what? And Marina hasn't turned up dead, hopefully not." I said.

"I'm thinking they may be taking the best from each club and the girls who don't like their intentions, are just whacked and they go elsewhere. I'm sending out my troops to all the strip clubs in town and warning them to be on alert."

73

Strip Club Murders

"Elaina said that she didn't send out anyone to talk girls into moving to her club. The first girl murdered was one of her own, although Elaina said she had quit. Could this be someone else, maybe a serial killer?"

"Anything is possible right now, we just need more facts. Speaking of that, are you still planning your little raid?"

"So far, yes, could be profitable or a bust, but at least we will know one way or another and can move on."

"Okay, keep me informed." He hung up and I put my head back on the couch after setting the alarm on my Palm, and took a nap.

Around 2 A.M., I called Buck and he said he was in my driveway. I looked out the front window and saw his Vibe parked off the side of the lawn. I was already dressed in my sneaky clothes, so went to tell Penny I was leaving. She mumbled something that sounded like leave me alone and I left.

We drove out, got to Mound Road, down to Heaven's Gate, and parked on a side street. We walked slowly to the club, it was dark and there were no cars in the lot. We walked around the back and I saw the wires going to the building, both electric and phone. We put on gloves so we didn't leave prints and Buck pulled over a small dumpster just below the phone connection. I jumped up, pulled out a pair of wire cutters, and snipped the line. I looked down at Buck and he opened the phone junction box and hooked up a small service phone and listened, nodding his head acknowledging the disconnect. I jumped down, we went to a small window, and I picked up a bucket sitting by the trash and smashed the window. I reached in and unlatched the thing and then we climbed in. Buck fell as he came in the window and crashed down on a table laid out with drinking glasses, he made enough noise to wake the dead. I came through and we walked through the building with just the light from our flashlights.

I found the office, because the sign on the door said office, I get paid the big bucks for my detective skills. It wasn't lock so we went in and there were no windows so I flicked on the lights. It was a nice office, clean, well laid out. A desk, four chairs, file cabinets and a small safe sitting in the corner of the room. Buck and I went through the desk and file cabinets, finding really nothing much. I stood looking at the safe, I had no skills in safe cracking, neither did Buck.

I knelt down to the safe and played with the dial just as a voice from behind us startled Buck and me. I fell back sitting on the floor, Buck stood up.

"You going to stare at it or open it?" said Earl, who was standing in the doorway. "Don't shoot, it's just me." He said holding his hands up.

"Shit. You scared the crap out of me." I yelled and got up. "What are you doing here and how?"

"I learned skills with the government, kind of a black ops thing. Don't ask; I'd have to kill you. I have abilities that would make ninjas blush."

"Fine, why are you here?" I was calming down now.

"I figured you two would need some help with the safe, I knew it was here from past break-in's that I had to investigate back when I was with burglary."

"Aren't you afraid of getting caught?"

"No, I'd just say I came in to investigate a break-in and found you two."

"Oh, so we go to jail and you're the hero."

Buck spoke, "Can we discuss this later and get the safe open?"

Earl went to the safe, did some magic to it, and about five minutes later, he had it opened.

"They teach you that in black ops too?"

"No, I trained with a former safe cracker who owed me, don't ask..."

"I know you'd have to kill me." I finished his sentence.

We went through the safe and pulled out papers and there were a couple of guns and a stack of cash.

I said, "Okay, we have a problem, if we take just the papers, Rex Erotica is going to be suspicious, so we would have to take the cash and guns too, make it look like a robbery, but what do we do with it?"

Earl smiled and said, "Well, an anonymous donation to the Detroit Homeless Mission would be nice."

I said that works for me, but we dump the guns; the homeless don't need them.

*

Chapter 11

We gather all the papers, guns and cash then Earl put them in a black cloth bag he pulled from his pocket. The man was definitely prepared. We looked around the room once more, checking behind pictures on the wall, when I saw something that made me wonder. I called Earl and pointed to a tiny black spot in the corner of the wall by the ceiling. I got up on a chair and looked closer.

"Yep, it looks like a lens, maybe hooked to a video." I reached up and pulled on it, the thing slid out from the hole in the wood and it was attached to wires. "Definitely a lens. We need to see where this goes."

The three of us went out and to the room next to the office and to the wall by where we saw the lens. The place looked like a storage room and I went to the shelves on the wall, I pulled some boxes off and found it. A video recorder that was running.

"Must be triggered by movement in the office." I hit the stop button and then ejected the tape and put it in my pocket. "We can look at this later, may have more evidence." I found about three other tapes and handed them to Earl, he put them in his black bag.

"I hope that was the only camera, we should have worn masks." I said.

"Yep, a real professional job you guys pulled." Earl smiled.

"Okay, black ops boy, let's get out of here." I said.

We slipped back out the window and I checked to make sure there was no evidence from our egress. I said we'd meet back at my office, it would be safer than a police squad room, I gave Earl the address and we departed. About thirty minutes later, we were in my office and Earl dumped out the contents of his bag on my desk. Buck sat back in the client chair and watched Earl and I go through the papers after I handed him rubber gloves to cover our prints in case. Earl said he'd take care of the guns, after having them checked against ballistics.

We piled the cash on another table and focused on the papers. I found mostly legal documents in the papers, things like the liquor license paperwork and titles to the building, made out to Rex Erotica Ltd. Earl came up with a journal type book and was looking through it. He showed it to me, there were women's names and descriptions of transfers to various clubs in New York. There were about three pages of names so far, I didn't see Marina's name.

We didn't find anything incriminating so I took the VHS tape from my coat pocket and went to the VCR next to my new TV. I turned it on and went to sit at my desk. I took the remote and hit rewind, back to where I figured our entrance was at. I hit play and we got a chuckle out of watching us trying to be good burglars. Earl said that we'd have to erase this part to be sure we didn't end up in jail. I rewound the tape back to the beginning of the tape and then we watched for the next hour before we shut it off.

There was enough evidence and conversations with various visitors to Elaina's office in regards to prostitution and forcing woman into sexual slavery, to send Elaina and her local people up for years.

"Unfortunately, there wasn't any mention of the parent company, none to take this to the Federal level to take down Rex Erotica. But we have enough to close down Heaven's Gate and their operation. We can contact New York police, and they can take it from there." Earl spoke.

"So, how do we take illegally obtained evidence to the DA?" I asked.

"Well, we pack up the tapes, along with the journal of names and guns, and put it in a bag with a note saying the burglars watched the tapes and felt it was their civic duty to turn it in. Remorseful crooks. I'll take in the bag and say I found it on the front steps of HQ." He smiled.

"Good, but first we erase our adventures," and I ran the tape to just before we came in and went to erase it.

Buck spoke finally, "Can't we copy our part so we have a memory of our first B and E?" He grinned. I just said I'd rather not have that memory or leaving evidence lying around.

I set it up to erase as I looked to Earl, "Doesn't it bother you to be breaking the law by joining us in our B and E?"

"Jim, before I took an oath to enforce the law as a cop, I did so many illegal things in the name of our government; I wore down my conscience long ago. You'd cringe if you knew some of the underhanded things that go on to protect our freedoms."

"You really were in some black ops thing?" Buck asked.

"You could call it that, the government calls it intelligence gathering and enforcement, and I spent time in both CIA and NSA. I did that for about twelve years, I was just out of high school when I started, before long I had enough of the underhanded way we did things. I just wanted to take down real criminals, so I joined the police. They wanted me to get into their special investigative branch; I said I just wanted to run the streets for a change." He said this rather sadly. "I've worked just about every aspect of being a cop; Vice, burglary, bunko, robbery and finally homicide. I'm happy now taking down murderers."

"A cop for all seasons." I said. "Ok, tape erased, let's make up our remorseful note and pack it up."

We worked on our plot for about another hour; we put the cash in another bag and Earl said he'd drop it off at the mission and then we closed it up for the night. It was now just after 6 A.M. and I was wearing down. Earl took the evidence package and the cash and went off. Buck asked if I needed him this morning, I said I was going home to take a nap and would call him. Buck and I drove out to my place where he left his car and then he drove off.

I went in and found Penny still sprawled out asleep on the bed, looking miserable. It was Saturday morning so Penny didn't have to work, thankfully. Willy was resting on his Bate's Motel chair, but watching me as I went out to the kitchen and then he popped up to eat the food I put down for him. I went to the couch and set my Palm alarm then lay down to nap.

I got about two hours of sleep when the phone rang and it was Earl. "Good Morning, how's my partner in crime?"

"Didn't you get any sleep?" I moaned looking at my watch.

"Nope I learned to take power naps, keeps me going without having to waste eight hours a day of my life."

"What's up?" I sat up now and saw Penny sitting at the snack bar eating what looked like oatmeal. She waved to me.

"Well, everyone at the station is ecstatic about the package our crooks dropped off this morning. The DA has been in and was fussing about where the bag came from, I did my best bold-faced lie about it and they are going to accept it, with trepidation, but it can go to evidence. They have sworn out arrest warrants for Elaina and the rest of her crew and we will be making a raid on the place when they open at noon. Want to be in on the fun?"

"Is Pamela Anderson a babe? Of course. Want me to come down to your office or meet you at the Gate?"

"You could just step out your front door and I'll drive you." He laughed. I went to the window and saw his Crown Vic with him waving to me.

"Why do people keep doing that to me? Come on in and meet my celebrity wife." I went and opened the door, just as Penny made a face at me.

"Sweetie, I'm not looking my best this morning to be meeting your little playpals." She moaned and ran to the bathroom.

I knew from experience that it would take her fifteen minutes to look radiant. Earl came up as I held the screen door for him and he came in. I motioned for him to sit on a chair and I sat across from him on the couch.

"So has Elaina discovered the break-in yet?" I asked.

"Not that we've heard of, she may have already arrived at the club, but then she may not even know it yet. Either way we are going to be there to mess up her day. I'm sure there will be a lot of lawyers running around the precinct today, the big New York kind. All screaming that their clients were set up and the evidence is not admissible due to its theft from the club. They can't prove it wasn't taken in the process of a burglary, which actually it was, but we can at least shut them down for a while until all the lawyers agree on what to do."

I said, "Yes, lawyers can be so annoying can't they. How do you find a lawyer in a tank full of sharks... the sharks are all jumping out of the tank."

**

Chapter 12

I said, "I just feel sorry for the girls whose jobs will be curtailed. I call Ron and see if he can fit some of them in his club."

"I know a couple club owners too, I'll talk to them." He said.

To the fifteen-minute mark, almost, Penny came out looking beautiful and refreshed. I introduced her to Earl and she said she hadn't been feeling well this morning, so she wasn't on her best. Earl said that she looked great and he was amazed that she even looked more beautiful than on TV. Penny blushed and I said that Earl needed glasses. Penny whacked me and said I could take a lesson from Earl in diplomacy. She said to go about our business and then she went off into the kitchen.

Earl winked at me and said quietly, "You're a lucky guy."

Penny yelled from the kitchen, "And he better remember that too."

Earl looked surprised and laughed. I said she has ears like a bat. I said that I wanted to freshen up and told Earl to be careful around Penny while I was gone; she's a bit crazy. Penny yelled that she heard that too. I went to the bedroom before she could get me. I was changed and cleaned up in about ten minutes, I don't waste time, and came out. Penny had Earl sitting at the snack bar eating toast. I came over, grabbed a piece off his plate, and munched it down before he could grab it back. Penny said for both of us to behave and then she said she was going back to bed to rest, we tired her out. I kissed her on the cheek and she went off.

"She isn't feeling well this morning, first time she's been sick since I met her. I'll tell you the whole story sometime." I offered.

"Well, we'll have a little time in the car on the way over to the Gate, tell me then, and I want all the sexy details." He stood and we went out to his car and

85

drove down towards Mound Road. He got on his cell and called someone to say he was heading to the Heaven's Gate and to have the men ready to go in. We had putzed away enough time at my home to get to the Gate just before opening.

"You copied the B and E video didn't you?" Earl smiled.

"You saw me erase the tape, how could I have done that?" I replied.

"You have an SD card recorder attached to your entertainment center. I watched you turn it on when you played the tape. You were good at covering it, but I'm trained to watch for such things." He smiled again, "I would have done the same thing, cover your ass." He laughed, "Can I get a copy too, for my entertainment and cover my ass?"

"I'll email you the file." I grinned.

We arrived at the Gate just before noon and there were a fleet of cop cars parked down the side street as Earl pulled up and circle the troops. He asked me to hang back in case of a gunfight. I said I would and we went to the front door.

They went in and Earl held up his badge as he entered the room followed by six uniforms, yelling this is a raid. Heckle and Jeckle put their hands on their heads, they knew the routine.

Earl headed down the hall and came to the office door; he could hear yelling in the office coming from Elaina. He pushed open the door and saw Elaina pacing in front of two large men standing by the safe and desk. Earl yelled Police and everyone to just stay still as the cops poured into the room. The two men held up their hands in surrender, Elaina gave a nasty look to Earl as he said he came back for a visit and to shut her down.

Earl walked in and looked around the room, "Gee, it looks like you're redecorating."

"You know perfectly well, we were broke into last night and robbed. I suspect you know something about it." She sneered as one of the uniforms cuff her at Earl's request.

"Elaina Ross, you are under arrest for kidnapping women subject to prostitution and in human trafficking. You know the rest, lawyer, right to remain silent, which you probably will. Say anything and it will be used to put you away for a long time. Blah, Blah, Blah." He looked to the uniform and said to do the Miranda properly; he was a little foggy on it. The cop smiled and gave her the correct reading.

The rest of the uniforms had rounded up the male workers in the building. I had come in now since I heard no gunfire and saw all the girls sitting at a couple of table looking upset. I came over as Earl walked down the hall and saw me. He came up as I was telling the six girls that I would try to see if I could get them relocated to other clubs and Earl gave me a thumbs up and told the girls he would help as well.

They brought out Elaina from the office and she gave me a dirty look as she went by. "I don't think she likes me." I said as Earl came up by me.

"You're second on that list, I top it. You haven't anything on Marina yet, do you?"

"Thanks for reminding me. I'm not sure right now what to think. No ransom demands, no threats, I was hoping that Elaina's files might have helped, but Marina wasn't even on the roster of women sent to New York. I hope you can beat it out of her, for Ron's sake. My only lead was this connection."

"Well, I'll do what I can to see if Elaina had anything to do with it. I can make concessions for her to get her statements on the big boys out in New York; I'll throw Marina in the mix to see if she gives." Earl offered and he said he had to go process and question her. I asked about the girls and he looked at them and yelled out loud, "Ladies, please come back here tomorrow around this time and I'll see what we can do for you. Take the day off, don't get in trouble, and we'll work it out." The women grumbled, but thanked us and then went out after us.

I wandered around the precinct while Earl had Elaina processed through booking and then had her taken to interview room A. He tracked me down and said to follow him. He pointed to the door to observation and I went in. I was alone at first, and then in came the DA observer, a woman this time. She nodded to me and I sat back watching Elaina in the interview room alone. I wondered where Earl was, probably getting a soft drink from the machine, making her wait around. The door to the room opened and Earl stuck his head in and looked at Elaina for a minute then went back out. Damn, psychological tactics, he was good. The door opened again and Earl came in asking if Elaina wanted a soft drink or water. She said nothing so Earl shrugged his shoulders and went back out. A few minutes later, he came back in with a cup of some liquid, and sat across from her, opening the folder he brought in, along with what looked like the journal we found in the safe.

"Morning Elaina, are you comfortable?"

"Screw you." She replied.

"Come on Elaina, and I was going to offer you such a sweet deal, why are you busting my balls?"

She was silent for way too long and Earl sat it out. Mr. Cool. She stared at him them asked what kind of deal. He smiled and leaned forward.

"Talk to me about your operation, everything from the girls being taken for prostitution to human trafficking, maybe if you can name some names or locations, I'll see if the DA goes easy on you." He went quiet again.

"What names are you talking about?"

"Oh Elaina, you didn't mastermind this operation, who leads the pack? Is it Rex Erotica? Talk to me."

Silence.

"Hmm... Slavery is a capital offense. I can't guarantee your freedom for this crime... unless you give us the higher ups. Of course, I still can't guarantee anything, that's up to the DA. But I'm sure we could work something out."

Silence.

"You know Elaina, I used to work for the government, and I can't say that I was involved in torture of prisoners, but we did manage to get scum to talk. I can't do much to you in the way of torture, I'm now a law-abiding police officer, but I'm sure your future prison mates aren't bound by the same code of law that I am. Do you value your life? Selling young girls out to be sex slaves to some wealthy Sheik. Turning girls out to do tricks against their will, not a good profession." He slammed his hand on the table causing Elaina to jump. "I don't like it! I got a young niece; I would do anything against the person who would turn her out, despite the badge." Then he said quietly, "I operate on a different system." He hit the table again, hard. "Are you hearing me Elaina?"

Silence.

"I'm offering you a deal to talk, want to make it miserable for yourself? Go ahead, no skin off my nose, but maybe yours."

She looked at Earl, "So what do you want to know."

**

Chapter 13

"Good, we are communicating now. Okay, your organization has been shipping women to New York to work as prostitutes, who is your contact?"

She looked around the room, her mind turning, uncomfortable she squirmed in her chair. I was sure she was afraid to name names, but prison could be worse. "If I give you names, I'm dead, but I do not want to go to prison either. How about witness protection?"

Strip Club Murders

"I'll work on it, you give us good info and it can be done. Whatcha got?"

She still paused, then, "Rex Erotica is just the tip of the thing. There's many hands in the mix below and I'd have to write down all the names involved. There are three men who handle the local connection; they take care of the details to get the women taken out to New York. The women are taken there to be held in houses for forced prostitution and some are shipped out for slavery overseas. The men here work out of an office in Southfield, on Eight Mile just past Southfield Freeway. They come in to my club to get prospects and they take it from there, but I keep track of names to be able to keep everything in order on my end." She said that as she noticed her journal on the table. "The men don't report back to me, they just take the women, I have no idea exactly how they transport the women, but I thought I heard they have a van to get them out there. I just supply the names, they do the dirty work."

I thought about the three men who came into Ron's club that could have been her goons.

"Is Rex Erotica connected with any Mafia family?" I sat up for that question as Earl threw it out.

"No, they're a new breed of Mafia, the business kind. A bunch of executives from a couple porn companies decided to make more money. They started Rex

Erotica and have the backing from many people, the kind that can be dangerous. But no mob connections, they have their own enforcers and hit men."

That relieved me and I could possibly talk to Angelo about this now. Then Earl brought up another good question.

"Elaina, do you remember a girl by the name of Marina Koska?"

"That's the name the private dick asked me about, I told him I didn't know her, I'll say the same to you. The three men did go around to other clubs, scouting the women; they may have grabbed her from her club."

I thought about the dead girl who worked at the Red Door Lounge, she was probably one of the unholy three's attempts that met with resistance from the girl.

Earl pushed over a pad of paper and pencil and told her to write down all the info she could and he turned to the mirror and winked.

About a half hour later, he had the list and came in to get me. Elaina was taken back to her cell; the DA lady went out and followed the guard escorting Elaina. Earl smiled at me and said, "All right, we can go get the three bears and find out what they know about the missing girls from the other clubs and hopefully your missing girl. While I was letting

Strip Club Murders

Elaina sweat it out, I got a report that there were two more women reported missing; they worked in two other clubs around the area. We may get a break here."

"Ron said the men looked like cops or Feds, but he didn't say they were knuckle busters." I offered.

"Well, I'm taking reinforcements along, so they won't be a problem." He made a call from his desk to arrange for a team to go with him and contacted Southfield police about his raid. He had already talked to the DA about a warrant and it was on the way. He looked at the pad again and noted the address Elaina gave him. "An office, these guys are fancy. When the warrant comes in, we rock."

We went to his office and sat waiting for the wheels of justice to process his warrant. "So how long have you been a cop?" I asked.

"About twenty years this next coming year. I've been chasing terrorists and criminals now for over thirty-two years, I'm happy to say I'm retiring in five. Maybe I'll start my own private investigation firm." He grinned at me.

"Fine with me, maybe we can join forces and work together. We could hire Trapper too, when he retires. The all old men investigation firm. We'll be in wheel chairs and following cheating spouses in our walkers." I laughed. "I don't really have any long range plans, I have a bit of money put away and Penny makes a fortune on her show so we would be comfortable, even when she leaves her show, but I think she'd go the distance until they force her to retire."

"I've watched your woman on the tube and I have to admit I've had sex thoughts about her." He said as if it was no big deal.

"I have to remember that if we invite you over again." I said.

"Is she good in bed?" He was still grinning.

"You're getting into dangerous territory here. I may have to tell you things you might not like to hear, for a single man. All I'll say is the girl is well endowed and horny. Two of my favorite things in life." I paused, "You aren't taping this to use against me are you?"

He laughed aloud and said no. "I wouldn't want to break up such a good marriage for my prurient interests."

"I have a question; you drove all the way from here up to my house just to drive all the way back down to the Gate, that's a long way for you to go, why?"

"I like to drive, and it gave me a chance to work things out in my head. Besides I want to get a look at Penny close-up, she makes great toast."

I laughed and said, "That is as far as you get to be near her, now I'm going to worry."

His phone rang and he answered. "Thanks, I'll come down and get it. Call the team and say we are go for it." He hung up and said, "The warrant was just delivered and we can go rescue a few women and hopefully Marina."

"I have to make a call to Buck, I forgot all about him, I'm sure he'll be pissed he missed all the action." I said.

"You can blame me for kidnapping you this morning." He smiled and went off to get his warrant.

I called Buck on my cell and I could tell he was still sleeping, even if it was just after noon. "Sorry to wake you but I have been a bit busy this morning. Earl came by and kidnapped me to go arrest Elaina and her crew, I'll tell you about it later. We are going out to Southfield and arrest the three suspects who may have been the ones who took Marina."

He said that was good and he had some more sleep to catch up on, between his flight from Vegas and our adventures the last couple days, he hadn't slept much. I knew that, my sleep system was in turmoil. I said

I'd tell him when we were back at the Detroit precinct if he wanted to watch the interrogation.

"Thanks, but you know my fear of police stations, I'll hang in till you are back at your office." He said, and I said I'd talk to him and we hung up.

Earl came back and motioned to me to follow. We went down to the motor pool and got his car out again. There were a number of patrol cars and one SWAT van ready and waiting for him. He waved and we all drove out to Eight mile and over past the Southfield Freeway. We pulled into the three-story office building and the cars all spread out around the front and the back, they covered the exits to be sure no one escapes. I was hoping that the girls would be held here and we might find Marina.

Earl slapped on his vest from his car trunk and handed one to me, but said to hang back. He went up to the front door and in with his troops following down the hallway to the office listed from Elaina's list. I stood by the entrance of the building watching down the hall as Earl opened the door to the office and the cops flooded in. The three men in the room were shocked to see so much hardware pointed at them, they put their hands up and surrendered. Hearing no gunfire, I came down the hall and looked in the door. The men were being cuffed and I heard Earl yell my name, I entered and went down the hallway in the office to a room at the end. I looked in and saw Earl cutting the restraints on one of four women tied up and sitting on make shift beds on the floor. The place was filthy and I came over to help release the girls.

"Jim, any of the girls here yours?" he asked.

I looked at their faces as I carefully pulled the tape from their mouths, "None look like her." I asked one girl if she knew of a Marina Koska. A blond turned her head to me, looking terrified, said she knew her; she was here. I asked where she was, the blond quietly said they already took her out this morning to New York.

**

Chapter 14

"Damn! Only a couple hours late. How was she taken out?" I asked the blond.

"Two men came in and took four girls that were also here, and said they only had room for four in their SUV. They'd be back for us tomorrow, they said. Thank you for rescuing us."

I looked to Earl as he asked the girl if she knew what the SUV looked like. The blond said no, they couldn't see it and the man just mentioned it as an SUV when he said he had no more room. The men were angry that there were more of us than they were told and he didn't like having to drive all the way back again. They argued with the three men here who kidnapped us. I was afraid they would kill us just so they didn't have to come back."

One of the other girls closest to the door said that she could hear them in the hall, and one man had said to put some boxes in the Navigator to take with the women.

"Okay, a Lincoln Navigator, that's better. If they are heading to New York, I can alert State Police from here to there to watch for two men and four women and stop every Navigator they see. They will most likely be heading out on the freeway, I'll have someone call New York state police and have them watch every road into the state and city." Earl was on his phone just after saying this. He talked to someone back at his precinct and related the story and the request to get a BOLO out and to call all state police between Michigan and New York about the car.

We helped the girls up and out of the room, it reeked of sweat and body order. Earl had called an EMS unit and they came in to look at the women. Southfield police arrived shortly after and said if they could help, they would. The three men were taken out to a transport wagon and back to Earl's station, as the EMS tech said the women were worn and tired but no adverse effects. Earl called a car and had the women taken to the station.

"Going to get crowded back at the office. Sorry about your girl, but the state police may still stop them. We can just hope." Earl said.

"At least I know she's alive, and somewhere on the road. That's a bit of a relief."

"The blond said she saw the clock on the wall in the hall when the men came to get the four, it was just before 10 A.M., so they've been on the road about three hours, hardly enough time to get to New York. We still may be good for the catch." Earl offered.

"Well, it's something I can at least tell Ron. Maybe I can see if Angelo and his connections can help."

"Going to involve the mob? Maybe we should wait and see what develops before starting turf wars." Earl warned.

"Yeah, you're right. But it's an option." I said.

"Well, I do like seeing the Mafia machine working for their pay. Yes, an option for later." He smiled.

"You know, you're scary." I smiled.

We left the office as crime lab techs were going over the office carefully. Earl's officers were taking boxes of files out to a police van to be taken back and gone over by his men. We had a ton of evidence to take care of the Michigan connection of Rex Erotica. All copies of evidence would be forwarded to New York cops to help nail the big boys out there. Earl and I drove back towards his station and I asked if we could take a side trip to the Side Door Lounge, he drove there.

We went in and was told Ron was in his office, Earl said he'd stay out to guard the women. I knocked on his door and he looked up, hopefully.

"Okay, I know where Marina is but we don't have her yet. She's still alive, we just need to stop the men who have her, but we have cops on it as I speak." I sat and then told him the whole story. He sat quietly and listened to me, then I finished and he smiled.

"She's alive, that's what I wanted to hear. Now we have to catch the bastards who have her." He said.

"We have the state police from about four states watching for the car, she's going to turn up, besides, they won't hurt her, she's too valuable to them. She's part of a larger crime, so I couldn't separate her from it to keep her low key about her citizenship, but I'm sure once the police stop the kidnappers, she'll be returned with no questions. Besides, I got Earl on my side now, I'm sure he'll help."

Earl popped his head in the door and asked if we were behaving. Ron asked him to come in and sit.

"Lieutenant, I want to thank you for helping to find my Marina." Ron spoke.

"We don't have her yet, so be patient and hope she'll be safe. These are dangerous people we're dealing with, human traffickers. They don't give a second thought about the women whose lives they ruin, just the money they'll make." Earl said.

"You don't think she could end up being sent out as a slave?" Ron asked.

"Well, they only have about four hours travel time, so she shouldn't have been yet." He looked to me and said he had to get back to the station to run the three men through the paces. We got up and said good-bye to Ron.

We got back to his precinct and he found the men were finished being booked and in their cells. He called to have them split up and put in interview rooms A to C. He sat at his desk as an officer came up with some paperwork for him to sign.

"We'll let them sweat in their rooms then I can go in and kick some ass." He smiled and I thought I saw a bit of the black ops agent in him, waiting for the torture to start.

Earl got word the men were in their respective rooms and one had demanded a lawyer, the other two remaining silent. Earl told the cop to put the lawyered up asshole back in his cell, and to be sure not to walk him into a wall a couple of times. The big cop smiled and went off.

We got up and went to the first room; I went into observation. There was no DA this time, maybe they would bring them in later. I also knew these men would have to be turned over to the FBI for kidnapping and interstate slave trafficking. I was surprised they weren't already here. Earl hadn't gone in yet, making the perp wait a bit longer. The interview room door opened and Earl looked in for a bit then went back out. I was seeing a pattern here. A few minutes later, Earl looked back in and asked if the perp wanted something to drink. He asked for water, Earl went back out. About five minutes later, Earl came back in with a cup of liquid and sat at the table, then he took a sip from the cup and set it down, opening the folder he carried in and read the paper inside before staring at the man for about a minute. The man squirmed a bit.

"You have been read your rights. This interview is being video recorded unless you have something to hide. Your name is Dan Fransen, correct?" The perp said nothing; Earl continued, "We arrested you in a place of business where women were being held against their will, bound and gagged and made to sit in a room for days until two, so far, unidentified individuals came and took four of the seven women in a Lincoln Navigator from the premises to be delivered to New York for the purpose of prostitution and or slavery. Is that about it?"

The man sat stoney faced, Earl slammed his hand on the table, hard, the perp jumped. "I'm sorry, would you like me to repeat that again?" Nothing. "Maybe I'll keep repeating it till you understand what I'm saying, I'm patient." Earl took another sip from the cup before setting it back down. The perp's eyes went to the cup and he looked thirsty. "Gee, did I forget your water, here you can have mine." Earl picked up the cup and dumped it on the table in front of the man. "You can lick it up like the dog you are." He growled. "Innocent women have had their lives turned upside down in pain and terror because you thought they would make a good sale to your cohorts in New York. Well, slimeball, we will get those men out there eventually. Now you can make it easy on yourself by saving us time and the expense of tracking down those people by cooperating and telling us who they are. I'm giving you first chance, we have your other two cronies in two other rooms, who will be the first to make a deal and get off easy. Who will go out heads up and the other two will slide down into the pit."

"I tell you and you can write my obituary. I'll have nowhere to run." He spoke finally.

"Well, Danny boy, we made a witness protection deal with Elaina Ross when she sang the blues. We can do the same for you, just tell us who are your New York contacts and those involved with the transport. Just a few simple names and you might skate. Or one of your buddies will, and you go to prison for a very long time. Tick, Tock, time's running out." Earl stood and slowly walked to the door, still looking to Fransen. He reached for the doorknob as Fransen gave in.

Earl came back to the table and pushed the pad and pencil to Fransen and told him to write down all the names and places in New York. Fransen began to write on the pad as Earl looked to the mirror and saluted me.

**

Chapter 15

"New York state police haven't been able to find the right Navigator, they've pulled over everyone they could find, and those were driven by everyone from little old ladies to a congressman, he wasn't happy, but fuck him. He will get over it." Earl said as he came into his office with me in tow. "It's been six hours and they should have arrived in the city by now. Not good."

"You have the list from Fransen, and the points of delivery for the women; we look there and save the women." I said.

"Are you suggesting a trip to New York?" Earl looked amused.

"I'm sure New York cops can handle it, but I'm not giving up on finding Marina and delivering her to Ron. Yeah, I'm going to New York, if I can take a look at that list Fransen gave you." I said.

He put the paper to the end of the desk and stood, "I need to hit the head, now don't be playing with any evidence on my desk, I'm warning you." He smiled and went out.

I picked up the list, looked out in the squad room, and saw the copy machine. I went there and ran the paper through it, grabbing up the copy and stuffed it in my pocket. I put the paper back on his desk, sat on the chair by his desk, and waited.

"I'm glad to see you've been a good boy." He smiled as he came back in the office, "Now, I stopped by the Captain's office and we had a quick heart to heart about delivering the evidence to New York, and we are good to go, if you need a driver."

"You knew we were going to be cleared to go, didn't you?" I asked. "So why make me sneak a copy of the thing?"

He smiled, "I just wanted to see if you could get to the copy machine, make your copy and get back here before I returned. You could be a great black ops agent." He laughed.

I rubbed my forehead with my middle finger and said, "When do we leave?"

"Well, if you want to bring Buck, I'd suggest you call him, and then go home to kiss your lovely wife and pack a toothbrush. We can leave around 5:00 after the car is packed with some of the most damaging evidence we got from the office."

"OK, I need someone to take me home since I was kidnapped from my house this morning." I said.

"I'll have one of our cars take you home, I have a lot of calling around to do before we go. This trip is meant strictly to take the evidence out to New York, you're traveling along is incidental, but the Captain says he understands your need to find your missing girl, but you're not official. Oh, and you'll have to sign a ride along waver saying you won't sue us if you get hurt. Not my idea, its policy."

"Fine with me, let's just get out there. I told Ron she was still alive and I want to see she is." I said.

Strip Club Murders

An hour later Buck was at my home as I was comforting Penny, who was still feeling sick. She was in bed and I set her up with a few comforts in the bedroom, putting everything near the bed, like the TV, phone and a cooler with ice packs, snacks and ginger ale.

"How long do you think you'll be out there?" she asked in a weak voice.

"I hope no more than a day or two. I'll call you when I can, but don't get freaked if I don't call every hour. I'll be with Buck and Earl and we will be joining the New York City police to investigate the criminals. So I'll be covered."

"Just don't shoot yourself with your own gun," she smiled and then turned green and barfed into the pail I put next to the bed.

"Crap, I hate to leave you."

"Go, so you don't get sick too, and rescue your missing stripper. But you will take me to the strip club when you get back and I'm feeling better."

"It's a deal, I'm sorry you're feeling bad, I'll call." I went out and gathered up Buck and we drove back down to Earl's precinct. I parked and we went to Earl's office and he was packing a few things into a gym bag.

"My emergency kit, always be prepared. The motto of us black ops. I had the evidence boxes loaded into a car that we will take and I called the New York police to expect us. They said they still haven't located the Navigator, it must have taken a different road rather than direct. Sorry." He said earnestly.

Earl continued, "We're going to take the scenic route around Lake Erie rather than going through Canada, it would be a hassle at the borders even if I am the police. Homeland Security and the Canadian border patrol people takes a dim view of our transporting weapons across the border through Canada. So we go around."

"That will add a bit of time to our trip won't it?" I asked.

He smiled and said to follow him. We went out to the motor pool and he pointed to a lean and low, midnight black, Dodge Charger police interceptor, a humming fast machine that would be our ride. It was a beauty and I could feel it vibrating with power even before I got in. Buck's jaw dropped and he drooled over the car. The motor pool techs had finished checking all the crucial parts of the car and gave it a good to go. We got in and Earl burned rubber once to show off in the parking lot, and then we drove out to go over to the freeway heading out to the eastern United States.

Strip Club Murders

Earl said he had evasive driver's training in the CIA, and drove formula one cars as a hobby, and we would be in New York before we even left the Michigan border. I said to just get us there safely, that's all I wanted. He laughed and called me a sissy girl. I said I'd slap his face, but he was driving.

Buck was stretched out in the back seat enjoying watching the scenery whizzing by and asked what the top speed was. Earl said it has been up to 160 but it could be pushed to about 180 if you were brave enough. Buck said to go for it, I said to go for half of it, Earl called me a sissy girl again.

Two and a half hours later and a few calls to local state police about our speeding through their areas in pursuit of the criminals, we flew across Interstate 80 heading toward New York, and arrived at the border of Pennsylvania and New Jersey. Earl saw a Jersey state police car parked on the side of the road ahead and stopped. We got out and the state cop stepped out of his car and met us half way.

"Howdy, Officer." Earl said as he flashed his badge. "You got the word on the Navigator with the kidnapped women in it."

The cop nodded, "Yep, you the one's from Detroit who are looking for them?"

"Yes we are, nothing going this way, eh?" Earl asked.

"I've been sitting her for the last three goddamn hours and pulled over two, nothing to write home about."

"Well, thanks for your help; we have a few leads in New York City as to where the women are being taken, so with the help of local cops we're bringing in evidence to crack the organization wide open. I saw you sitting and wanted to take a breather and say howdy."

"Nice ride y'all got there. What's under the hood?"

"It's the pursuit package, 426 Hemi and tweaked out to run fast. It's a nice ride as you say." Earl looked to me and said we needed to head on, thanked the cop again and we got back in the car and drove off. "Always good to keep in touch with the local cops in case of trouble." He said to me with a smile. I thought of Trapper and his same words of advice when I was going out to Vegas for the first time with my Glock.

We drove through New Jersey and I was trying to follow the map but it was a bit of a mess to figure, all the highways going everywhere, but Earl said he knew where to go. I asked if they gave training in black ops for reading road maps, he laughed and said they taught him how to follow the signs. We got to the western New Jersey-New York state border at Weehawken, found the Lincoln Tunnel, and drove through into the great island of Manhattan.

Strip Club Murders

I'd never been in New York other than a layover while flying through Kennedy Airport on the way back from Germany after they let me out of the army in 1971. We drove around; Earl did seem to know where to go. We drove up Ninth Avenue to West 54th Street and Earl found the Midtown precinct where Earl was told to go with the evidence.

Earl pulled into a space in front of the building with a sign saying "Police Car Parking Only"; Earl smirked and said we were in a police car weren't we. We got out and a couple of the officers standing in front of the building were eyeing the Charger. Earl flashed his badge and before we went into the building, he asked the officers if they had valet parking, it got a smile from them. Earl, Buck and I went into the building and found our contact, Detective Captain Lou Brege, of the Organized Crime Unit, waiting to greet us.

**

Chapter 16

Earl introduced us, then Brege said, "Gentlemen, welcome to New York. I'm Captain Lou Brege of OCU and I'm expecting some good evidence to shut down these bastards. We got bupkis on them, as they have been on the up and up about their business dealings. They have hidden the crimes real well, so you say you got some goods on them." He looked anxious to deal.

Brege was a rather large, African-American, built with a neck almost as big as his head; his chest was round and firm looking, unless he was wearing a Kevlar vest under his clothes. He sported a goatee and had shaved his head; it gleamed under the florescent lights. He was dressed in a good-looking tailored suit that fit his frame and had a bearing to him that said 'I'm the man', which I'm sure he could back it up.

Earl spoke, "We closed down a delivery conduit from Detroit dealing in prostitution and human trafficking being toward a focal point of your fair city. This morning we closed down a strip club involved in recruiting women against their will and then we closed the transfer point shipping the women to here. Our search found half to the captive women, the other half are in the Navigator everyone is looking

113

for. We raided the office and got lots of goodies you may be interested in. The files are in our car."

"Have the Feds been informed about the kidnapping and interstate trafficking?" Brege asked.

"Well, Captain, we wanted to see where this all was going before we waste their precious time." Earl smiled.

Brege grinned remembering a number of his cases being pulled from him by the Feds. "Okay, but we got about a day before they can cry foul. I don't want them sniffing around messing up my investigations. I like the Feds when they mind their own business. Let's get your stuff in here and go over it."

Brege grabbed a couple of uniforms and we went out to the car to get the files. Brege let out a long, low whistle when he saw the Charger, "They issuing these suckers to cops in Detroit now?"

"Well, it is the Motor City. We go all out for our reputation." Earl smiled wide.

"Damn, we need to update our rep." He looked to the uniforms he brought out, "Now that's the kind of patrol cars I want for my men." He told them to get to work as Earl opened his trunk. The uniforms were taking the three boxes out of the trunk and back into the building. Brege had a room set up for the OCU to go over the files and see if they had anything tying into their turf. Brege had brought in four of his men and had them divide up the papers and go through them. He asked us to sit in the cubicle he set up as his temporary office. "OCU is not housed here; we're here because most of the offices of Rex Erotica are located nearby. So we're setting up nice and close to the action."

I asked, "Have there been any sightings of the Navigator coming in with the kidnapped women?"

"Sorry, but they seemed to have vanished or took a longer route to get here. But we're on the watch for them. Please understand, Lincoln Navigators are in abundance around Manhattan, we can't stop every one of them, but we're watching for the right people in them."

I thanked him and sat back. I looked to Buck sitting off to the side; he wasn't so much bothered being in this cop shop since he wasn't well known here. He felt safe.

Earl asked us if we were hungry, I realized I hadn't eaten all day and said I could use something to eat. "Captain, where would you recommend a good place to get some genuine New York food?"

The Captain smiled and told Earl a couple of places nearby, so we went to the closest one and had a good meal.

Strip Club Murders

After I ate, I called Penny and she sounded so miserable, I felt really bad. I told her I wasn't having much luck here so far but the day isn't over yet. She said she wanted to go back to sleep and told me to call again later. I gave her a smooch on the phone and hung up. I asked Earl if he had an expense account for this trip.

"Hell, no, I'm lucky I got the department to pay for gas for the Charger. We're on our own here." He laughed.

"So we have to pay for our own motel too?" I said.

"Yep, no Ritz-Carlton for us, maybe a Motel 6, if we can find one." Earl said.

"And we split that cost too, I suppose." I said.

"Of course, I provided the transportation, but not the motel." Earl laughed.

I looked at my watch and said, "Well, the girls would have to be here by now, unless they stopped somewhere in between for the night."

"It's very possible they did. I don't think they run by a schedule, maybe they stopped at some motel along the way." Earl said.

"It would be risky, wrangling the women into a motel all tied up. Might make for some embarrassing questions by the motel management." I offered.

"Yeah, they are probably here by now. We'll just have to be patient."

"We get too patient and Marina is deep into the bowls of prostitution, or worse, being taken out of the country." I said.

Earl's cell phone rang, it was Brege, Earl gave him his number in case. "Hello?" He listened for a bit then hung up.

"He said he had enough names and places to get warrants on the offices of Rex Erotica. He asked if we wanted to tag along. You guys up for it?" We paid our food bill and went back to the station house. Brege said the warrants hadn't come through yet; it's a slow process here, getting the DA to find time to track a sympathetic judge and get him to sign. We would just have to wait.

Brege looked at me, "You're a P.I. eh? What's your interest in all this?"

"I was hired to locate a missing girl and it turns out she was taken from our location and brought here in the same Navigator you're watching for. I made a promise to her boyfriend that I would get her back safe and sound."

"I'm gonna be honest with you, if we don't find her in the next twenty-four hours, she can easily disappear into the city slime. You may never find her." He wasn't smiling.

"I thought of that. But I'm persistent." I said.

Earl told Brege that I was a real hound dog when it came to big time killers and mentioned a couple of the more noteworthy cases I had. Brege said he had heard of the cheerleader and Bridezilla cases and looked at me with a little more interest.

"I can't take credit for it all; I had a lot of good police help from both Michigan and Las Vegas."

Brege asked if I knew Captain Weber out in Vegas, my mouth must have dropped and he laughed. "I take that as a yes. I knew Weber from back when I lived in Reno. We went through police academy together. "

"I'll have to tell you about our adventures with him on my last trip out. He's quite a guy." I said.

"He is, but he's a little too nervous." Brege said and I agreed.

"Captain, do you anything know about the Traviano family?" I asked.

"Oh hell yes, one of my favorite families; don Traviano just got married to Francis Mangelo, an aging Mafia princess from a former New York crime family relocated to Mississippi, now back here since the wedding. Why do you ask?"

"I was at their wedding in Vegas chasing down the Bridezilla killer and one of Francis' wiseguys helped me out greatly in finding and capturing the killer. His name is Angelo; I never did get his last name. Know him?"

"Angelo DeMarco, he's the top man in Francis' army, a real sweetheart. If you're friends with Angelo, you got a friend forever. A dangerous friend, but a friend never the less. We're ninety percent sure the Traviano family is in numbers and illegal gambling, but they don't participate in prostitution or drugs. don Traviano has a real dislike for sex for money and getting people strung out. He figures gambling is a man's sport and if they lose their shirts, they deserve it. His family is low on our radar; we just want the hard-core peddlers. You have any connections to the Travianos?"

"Not really, I just met Francis and Angelo, so that's as close to the family as I got. I'm working on finding the missing girl for a cousin of Angelo's; it was through Angelo that I got the case."

"Well, I hope Angelo doesn't bring any of his men in if he finds out his cousin's girl is here in New York.

We don't need that kind of help, but off the record, sometimes I would like to see the right kind of hit, especially against Rex Erotica." Brege said.

"Well, Angelo's cousin knows that she's here, but he doesn't want Angelo involved, he doesn't want bloodshed either."

"Smart man. My Organized Crime Unit has enough to fill their days without getting involved in a gang war."

One of Brege's men came in and said they had the warrant. Brege stood and said, "Let's go bust some ass."

**

Chapter 17

Everyone went out to their vehicles, being joined by SWAT already in their van and ready to go. Buck, Earl and I got into the Charger and waited to see where everyone was heading, then followed them out. Earl pulled in behind the SWAT van figuring it was harder to lose sight of in the traffic. We drove around a few streets and up to a four story building looking like it was built in the 1800's, or an amazing replica of early New York architecture.

The team all piled out and up to the door of the building. The door was locked, so they brought the door ram up and smashed it in. Buck and I held back, Earl diving right into the building, until we didn't hear any gunfire. We went in and heard a lot of yelling, so we followed the sound, down to an office where we could see three men with hands in the air as the NYPD cops started to cuff them. There was a brunette woman sitting at a desk looking frightened, she looked like she might be a secretary, as Brege and his men went in through some fancy walnut doors to another office. Earl was behind them and looked back to us, smiled, and he waved us to follow, we did.

There were two men in the office standing at their desks and yelling about this being an illegal raid on his office. Brege pushed the search warrant at him and said to read it and weep. He did and started to reach for his phone, Brege placed a huge hand on his and said with a growl, "I wouldn't do that. You can call your lawyer from jail."

The man protested as Brege's men cuffed them, and took them out. I went around the offices looking in rooms, already searched by the cops, hoping to find a bunch of kidnapped women along with Marina, but no luck.

Earl was talking to the secretary as Brege came up. I walked over to hear what Earl was asking.

"Miss Davis, how long have you worked here?" He asked after looking at the nameplate on her desk.

"About six months, I was hired through a friend of Mr. McKinley, the owner of the company, the one you took out of here." She tried to smile at Earl, but Brege's imposing figure lurking behind him made her uncomfortable.

"How much do you know about this business?" Brege asked.

"It deals with sexual videos, um, you know porn..." she seemed to be wanting to say more but hesitated, "I don't approve, but it's a job. This economy is really bad, so I had to take what I could get."

"Do you have a catalog of the videos handy?" Earl asked. She reached behind her and took one off of the pile on a table and gave it to Earl.

"Okay, a delicate question, do you know of any dealings your bosses have with prostitution?" Earl asked.

"Oh, no, they aren't into that kind of thing, just the made up stuff on the videos." She managed a smile.

Bob Moats

Earl was looking through the catalog and he seemed a little too interested in it. "Does this company have a warehouse where the videos are stored?" He asked as he kept flipping through the book.

"Uh, yes, um, it's about two blocks from here." She was nervous.

Brege asked, "Is the warehouse under the Rex Erotica name, owned by Rex Erotica?"

"Oh, yes, it's all part of the company." She was smiling at Brege now.

"Any other properties that you know of?" Brege was talking now, as Earl wandered towards us with the catalog, still perusing it.

"Well, yes, they own about ten clubs where they do exotic dancing... Okay, it's stripping. Oh, hell, they own strip clubs." She looked like she had changed from Miss Manners to the bawdy Miss Bette Midler. "They are whore merchants, the whole lot of them. They have dealings like you wouldn't believe. Carnal palaces, sex clubs, bondage and fetish, if it has to do with a woman's body, you name it, they do it." She folded her arms and sat back. Earl about broke his neck turning his head to face her as she let out her little tirade.

"These bastards have paraded around all these young girls, some I don't think are even old enough, to be molested by these degenerates that come through like it's a sporting event." She pouted, and went silent. We all waited to see if she had more to say. She didn't.

"Do you know anything about human trafficking of women from Michigan?" I asked from a distance.

She turned her head to me and said, "They come from everywhere. Michigan, Ohio, Illinois... all the sweet little innocent girls from the Midwest, they like those kind here."

"Kidnapped or recruited?" Brege asked.

"I don't know they don't talk to me, just in and out."

"Any come in today from Michigan?" I asked hopefully.

"Yeah, arrived earlier this afternoon, they were taken to any one of the ten clubs they own. There are a number of the clubs that have private back rooms for sex. You have to have a lot of dough and they check you out carefully to be sure you aren't a cop."

Earl asked if she had a list of the clubs and she opened a drawer and took out a paper that was her phone list to the clubs and it contained the addresses. Earl went for it but Brege grabbed it up and said to Earl, "Let's not be playing cowboy here. You go storming these places without a warrant and we could screw up."

"Yeah, but I'm not a cop here, I'm a citizen just wanting to have a little fun while I'm here on vacation." He smiled. "Besides I want to show my friends here a good time on the town." Motioning to Buck and me, neither of us looking like cops.

Brege smiled and said, "If we get a warrant and start raiding the first club, the next nine will have shut down faster than a greyhound on a rabbit's ass. Maybe if you guys just nosed around first, it might help."

"What about the raid here, won't that get out to the clubs?" I asked.

"These video porn houses are raided on a regular basis. Just to let them know we are doing our jobs. I'll talk to the Rex Erotica bosses, as if we got complaints about obscenities in their videos. Then we'll hold them over night while you good citizens do your exploring, before they can shut down. If there is any underground prostitution or sex clubs, I want to know. Keep a list of each club and report back to me."

Brege put the list back on the desk and asked the secretary if she would join him downtown to make her statement, and they left. Earl picked up the paper and looked to Buck and me. "Want to go hit a couple of strip clubs?"

Buck let out a small whoop and we went out. Sitting in the car Earl was looking at the list, I asked for the first address, he read it off as I went into my Palm TX map program for New York City and surrounding area and found the location. He looked at my Palm and said he liked it. We drove over to the club as I navigated and pulled into the parking area next to the building. The club was called the Purple Passion and the building was painted purple. Lights flashed around the front marquee proclaiming 20 beautiful girls all dancing for your pleasure.

"I've died and gone to heaven." Buck announced.

"Buck, I doubt they have strip clubs in heaven, you may have to go the other way for that kind of entertainment." I said to his comment.

"Well, then I'll just have to be bad to get there won't I?" He smiled.

We went to the door and into the barely lit entrance, but as soon as we opened the inner door, we were assailed by sound and strobing lights of all colors. We approached the bar and grabbed our stools as a barely dressed female bartender came over and took our orders. It was now just before 7 P.M. and I wasn't driving, so I ordered a beer and of course, Buck asked for a Diet Sprite. The woman stared at Buck as if he were crazy and he said he was on the wagon. She brought him a regular Sprite and said he may be on the wagon, but he was too tough looking to drink sissy diet pop. Buck laughed out loud and the woman winked at him and wiggled her cute butt as she went off. It wasn't hard to watch, but it made Buck hard I'm sure.

Earl looked around, "Okay scouts, what is our plan of attack?"

"I guess we could ask for the special of the day and see what we get, I guess, I've never requested a prostitute before. Have you?" I said.

"I've had my share." He boasted.

A dancer was walking by and I flagged her down, she smiled and came to me. "Hi, my friends and I are in town from Michigan, do you know where we can have a little more fun?"

"Let me see your driver's license. All of you." She asked like it was something she'd said many times before.

I paused then took out my wallet and showed her the license. She looked at mine, Buck's and Earl's and said, "Okay, follow me." We picked up our drinks and walked behind her, I was watching her thong running up her butt crack and wondered if it hurt. She took us toward the back of the club and through beaded curtains into the back half of the main room. There were plenty of easy chairs and a couple of couches that were occupied by men being ridden by nearly naked women, giving lap dances. I stopped her.

"I was thinking a little more fun than this." I said.

She stood looking at Buck, then Earl, and me then she said, "How much?"

"Aren't we supposed to ask that?" Earl asked.

"I mean how much fun, dork." She snapped back.

"Ah, yes, we'd like our wicks tweaked." Earl responded and winked.

The girl stood for a second then said, "Any of you guys cops?"

"Do we look like cops?" I asked, carefully wording the answer.

She paused again and then told us to follow. We went to the back wall, through a curtain, and up to a door that she knocked on. There was a small flap in the door that opened inward and a pair of eyes peered out.

I expected her to give the password, but she didn't, the door opened and we went in.

Chapter 18

We went down a flight of stairs into a room that reminded me of a big locker room. The walls were all covered in those pale blue square ceramic tiles you'd find in a locker room, and I was waiting to walk into the shower room, but found none. The women were all lined up around the room and some were walking off with men who selected them, I had no idea where they were going. Earl latched on to a tall leggy blonde and they went off somewhere. I thought, great, our back up has deserted his post.

Buck was in a state of shock with all the flesh surrounding us and I had to tell him to close his mouth. I didn't really want to indulge in sex for hire, I didn't care if Buck did, he was a single guy and even though he was Maria's "boyfriend", I wasn't going to deny him the pleasure. There was an older woman, probably the madam, walking around yelling at men to make up their minds and pick a girl. She came by us and asked if we were buying or looking. I said back off, my money is just as good now or later and she made a face and walked off to yell at some young guys who probably were too young to be in here. This place had no age limit I was sure.

Strip Club Murders

We walked around as I was hunting for Marina and didn't see her. We had seen all the girls and waited around for the ones who went off with men, to come back. A short time later, Earl came flying through being pursued by the madam, he yelled that he'd meet us outside, and ran up and out. Buck and I had seen enough and we went out the way we came in.

Outside we met up with Earl who was laughing by the car. "What happened to you?" I asked.

"I went with the girl to see where they go for the sex act; they have these tiny rooms in the back with one bed and nothing more. The girl sat on the bed and asked what would I like. I said I just wanted to talk and she said that would still be $50 and I said I didn't have any money. She started screaming for someone named Linda and that crazy woman came in and chased me out."

I held back a laugh, but it wouldn't be subdued. Buck was already laughing and then we got in the car, wrote down what we found here and looked up the next address, and drove there.

Same set-up, different place. We went in, did our just-in-town-dumb-tourist act, and found basically the same layout as the first. This time Earl scouted out the place without molesting any of the girls, Buck wanted to participate but he held back, we didn't have a lot of time to scout out ten clubs looking for Marina.

The fourth club we came to refused us anything more that stripping and lap dances. One girl referred us to another of their clubs for what we wanted. We made note and went to the next club. It was called Ladies' Delight and they advertised out front that they had over 50 dancers available. It was a huge club, about three of any of the other clubs could fit in it, so it wasn't as easy to seek out one woman in the place, but we tried. Our dumb tourist act worked well here, we were escorted to a rather nice looking section of the building that was set up to look like a Victorian cathouse. I figured lots of money would talk here; I had brought enough cash with me to cover any emergency, including a motel room, which we hadn't found yet.

We wandered through the women available and didn't find Marina. I asked the woman who seemed to be the madam in charge if they had any Russian women available. She said they had a new group of women that came in today and there was one Russian beauty with them. I asked if it were possible to see her, the madam said the girl wasn't ready to start in this club, maybe tomorrow. I said I would be back and gave the madam a fifty-dollar bill and asked her to remember me, she smiled and said she would.

We went out and Earl looked at me and said, "You gave her a fifty?" I said I wanted to impress on her the importance of my needs. He just shook his head and said let's move on. I said this is the club we will be back to, if the madam was right about the Russian beauty.

We hit the rest of our list, not finding Marina in any of them, and it was time to find a place for us to crash for the night. It was now late, around midnight, and I really wanted to have a nice hotel room with a good view so we tracked down a Hilton Hotel and I paid for it. We were shown to our room and they had to bring in extra beds for us. I insisted that since I paid, I got first choice of beds and took the master bedroom and I was sleeping alone. Earl and Buck took the day beds in the main room and both grumbled about the treatment. I yelled out to them, that they could pay for their own room or go to a cheap motel, otherwise, shut up. They did. I took a nice warm shower, crawled into the king-size bed, and then called Penny.

It was after midnight and I was sure I would wake her, but I had to say good night. She answered after the third ring and I said hi. She said, "Oh, it's just you."

"Thanks for the excited greeting. I just crawled in bed here and thought of my poor suffering baby back home all alone."

"I'm not alone, I have a few men friends over to keep me warm," she answered.

"Any one I would know?" I asked.

"Nope, they're all strangers I picked up at a local bar. They're all foreign exchange college students here to study sexual habits of lonely women."

I started singing Elvis' song "Are You Lonesome Tonight", she said to stop or she would hang up. I stopped.

"Have you overdosed on naked women yet?" She asked.

"I've seen enough to last a while, but I still prefer your naked body." I said diplomatically.

"Smart man, did you find your missing person?"

"No, but I feel I'm getting closer. Had one good lead today, a madam said they had a Russian girl come in today but she wasn't ready to enter their domain. So we're going back tomorrow to see if it's her. I'm hoping for the best."

"Well, I hope you succeed. Then you can come back and nurse me. I'm so ill without you."

"Poor baby, I'll be back as soon as possible. Now you go back to your students and don't be rude to them." I smiled.

"Me, rude? I'm not rude to anyone but you, as you know well enough."

"Yes, I do know so well, now get some sleep and I'll call tomorrow, hopefully with good news. Good night, babe." She said good night and we hung up.

I laid back and thought about my little over a year with Penny, all the things we went through. Her kidnappings, twice, and how I felt. It scared the hell out of me to think that my occupation could cause her great harm. She was stronger than she let on, she could handle herself as I saw during the kidnappings, when she bashed the heads of her kidnappers with those lead pipes, I had to chuckle at the memory. It bothered me that I was out here in New York about 700 miles from her, nosing around dangerous areas that could get me killed if I stuck my nose out to far. Back home there have been many nights I lay in bed thinking these thoughts of my job and wondering why I do it. Then I think about the look on Ron's face when I told him that Marina was still alive, and the hope he had expressed that I'd find her. It made it worth the effort. But I know I couldn't put up with the look on his face if I came back without her. It spurred me on to do the job I accepted. Tomorrow I would have more time to find her, with or without my little crew. Earl had something about him that I knew I could trust, even if he had a dark past, it could be useful. Buck was willing to go into hell and back out with me, so I knew I could depend on him to watch my back. I had a good team.

I thought about maybe looking up Angelo while I was out here and saying hi to Francis, if I could get near her. Just a subtle visit to say hi and ask how's the mob doing?

**

Chapter 19

Morning came after a good night's sleep, one I hadn't had in a long time. Maybe the mattress had something to do with it or maybe because Penny wasn't bouncing all over me. Either way I slept well. I looked out and found my two friends still sleeping, Earl was just in his shorts lying on his stomach, he had a number of large, ugly scars on his back, maybe from his secret agent days? Buck was flat out on his back with his mouth wide open but no sound coming out. I had to watch to see if his chest moved to prove he was breathing. He was. I went back into the bedroom and looked out the window at the city. It was like all the pictures I had seen of New York, beautiful and filled with huge buildings. I thought about calling room service but I decided to wait for Buck and Earl to get up before I called.

A half hour later, the two of them were sitting up, and I asked if they wanted something for breakfast.

Strip Club Murders

Earl declined anything to eat, but said he would take a gallon of coffee, Buck said whatever I was having would be good for him. I called and ordered up and they had the food and coffee to the room in about another half hour. Buck and I ate; Earl drank down the pot of coffee as if he was a man lost in the desert. I was waiting for the caffeine to kick in on him, as I dressed and got ready for the day.

I came out of the bedroom, Earl was sitting at the little writing desk provided with the room, and he was busy making his report for Brege, detailing all the clubs we visited and what he had observed. That would be good for warrants to go in and close them down, but I hoped we'd find Marina before they did. Although any raids would have netted Marina in the pack and we could pull her out, but I didn't want to have her exposed to a lot of questions by the NYPD. I went back into the bedroom to get my toys to go out and fight crime.

"Earl, why doesn't Brege have his own men to go check out the clubs to close them down? Why let us do it?" I asked as I came out of the bedroom suite.

"Brege is with OCU, organized crime, not vice, but this case laps over to the clubs if it involves Rex Erotica. Don't ask me why Vice is taking a blind eye to their prostitution, maybe their men are too well known to go snooping and we can prove we aren't from around here. Ask them." He replied.

"Well, I want to go back to Ladies Delight and see if the Russian beauty they have is Marina and get her out of there. I registered this room for one more day in case we don't find Marina and get to leave today, and I get the big bed again." I said, and they didn't complain.

We waited until about 10 A.M., went back to Midtown Precinct, and found Brege in his makeshift office. He smiled at us and said they were going to hold on to the Rex Erotica bosses as long as they could stall, but their lawyers were starting to circle. He asked what we had, and Earl gave him the paper he worked up this morning. He smiled as he read the list and made a call to someone he called Ralph, and told him he had the goods on Rex Erotica's strip clubs. He paused to listen and then said he had a list of what went on in each club, from investigations by a Detroit Police Lieutenant who brought out the evidence from Detroit that Rex Erotica may be into prostitution. He said they had no proof yet as to any slavery, that's going to be something needing more investigating. He made small talk then hung up.

"The city of New York appreciates your help in this matter. These clubs weren't really suspected of hooking on the side until you brought up the evidence against them. All this time, and vice hasn't looked into them. Maybe something is a bit off in Vice." He went quiet for a bit. "Well, that's something I'll have to look into later. Now, have you found your missing girl?"

I answered, "We had a good lead on that, one madam said they had a Russian female come in yesterday, but wasn't ready to work the club. We're going back today to see if it's her. I'm hoping for good luck."

"We aren't going to be jumping on this right off, we put the Rex Erotica secretary in protective custody under the premise that she had a prior warrant for her and is being held for further questioning. That keeps her away from McKinley, her boss, and what she told us yesterday. We decided to let them all go, and then we'll watch them so we can get the whole shebang tied up. Now they may be a bit worried about our attack on them, so they may try to make some changes in their operation, which makes them more exposed." Brege said.

"Do you think they may shut down operations and disappear?" I asked.

"Ah, hell no, they have too much money involved. What they have already invested and what they would lose if they shut down. No, if they think we aren't on to them for the prostitution and slavery, they'll keep right on doing what they do well."

"Just a question, you're with organized crime, these guys aren't the mob, and doesn't Vice take care of prostitution cases?" I asked.

"Fair question, but these guys are a new kind of organized criminals. Businessmen with an agenda. They may not be mob connected, but they are organized in their own little world. They have been adding more enforcers and we believe they may be branching out to gambling and drugs. That means if they do, we will have friction between them and the real Mafia. Not a good prospect and something I don't want to see in my town." Brege replied. "A bunch of idiot businessmen thinking they know more than the mob, who have years of experience on them, and more ruthless killing power. The only thing I give these men is that we believe they may be bringing in mercenaries as enforcers."

Earl perked up and said, "I still have a little pull in the governmental circles, let me see if I can find out what the word is on unauthorized troop movements. I know a guy who keep a list of mercenaries. It's his hobby." He smiled.

"It would help; I hope we can stop these scums before we have a full blown siege on the city. Please be careful out there." Brege said as a uniformed officer came in and said the lawyers were screaming and wanted some action.

Brege smiled, stood, and said, "I hate lawyers. Excuse me," and went out.

Buck was seated on a chair off the side and I was sitting next to Brege's desk. Earl was sitting on the large window ledge, pulled out his cell phone, and dialed. After a few, he smiled and said, "Morry, you're a horse's ass." He listened, and then continued, "Yes I know I am, I need some info, how are you set up on names of recent mercenaries out for hire?" He paused again, then continued, "Okay, Rex Erotica out of Manhattan in New York, they may be hiring bad men and I need to know if you can dig anything up for me. Yep, I'm still a cop in Detroit... Yeah, it's a living... Sure, it would be a real help, I'm in New York right now and Rex Erotica is forming their own little gang, possibly to push out the mob families here. See what you can find, I'll owe you. Yeah, anything I can afford, but I don't get you any women." Earl smiled and hung up.

"Must be nice to have the government in your speed dial?" I smiled.

"Just have to know the right people. Shall we go get some food in our stomachs and then to Ladies Delight to rescue a damsel in distress." He stood and headed out of the office, followed by Buck and me. On the street, we found a small open deli and had sandwiches as we sat watching New York citizens pass us by, while we sat on the seating out front of the building.

"In Michigan, if we sat outside a deli, we'd probably be rained on or suffer from gray sky depression." I said.

"You're being too hard on Michigan; there are just as many sunny days as are there cloudy days. I know a couple of nice delis in the city with outdoor seating; I've been to them a number of times." Earl said.

"I'll still will take Las Vegas for the constant sunshine and heat any day over Michigan's cold and gloom." I countered. Buck agreed with me.

As we sat and talked we watched a purse snatching in progress, Earl stuck his foot out and tripped the perp and pulled his gun on him, warning him not to move. "Now here's something you don't see every day in Michigan." He smiled.

**

Chapter 20

The woman whose purse was snatched came running up, thanking Earl for his heroics. He smiled and handed her the purse and she started to walk away. "Lady, don't you want to press charges?" He yelled, she yelled back saying she was late for a meeting and went off. Earl had the snatcher by the collar and looked at him, "I don't really have time to fill out paperwork, you are damn lucky this time, but if I see your sorry ass on these streets again, I may plaster you with paper, understand slimeball?" The young man nodded hard and Earl let him go, he skittered off.

"Damn people, always in a rush, sure let the criminals go, that'll teach them a lesson." Earl grumbled. "In Detroit that same woman would be beating on the perp with her umbrella." He smiled now.

Buck and I sat laughing; we finished eating and went back to our car. We drove out to where the Ladies Delight was and since it was now just after noon, the club was open. We went in and had to go through the process to be sure we weren't cops and were taken back to the Victorian cathouse. The same madam was there and she smiled when she saw me. Earl asked if I had another fifty to give her, I just said to shut up.

"I see you remembered me, has the young Russian girl arrived?" I asked as we approached her.

"I'm sorry sir, but she hasn't been indoctrinated to our club yet, maybe later this evening. Isn't there someone else you'd like to try?" She asked.

"No, I had my heart set on Russian. Thank you and we'll be back." I said but didn't give her a tip this time, maybe she'd have Marina in the next time we come in and then she may get tipped. We left and Buck asked what do we do now?

"Well, if you'd like a tour of the city, I can do that." Earl offered.

"You evidently have been here before?" I asked.

"Oh, yeah, I had some work to do for the United Nations, can't say what, but I spent a couple weeks here." He gave us a wide grin.

"You're just so full of experiences aren't you?"

"I could write a book, but there are people in high offices who might not like that." His grin widened even more.

"Okay, give us the nickel tour." I said and we went to our car and drove off.

Earl ushered us all around the city, I was confused as to where we were but he knew the town. We saw the Statue of Liberty, Madison Square Gardens, drove by the Empire State Building and cruised up Broadway and around Times Square. It was a sight to see. We didn't have a lot of time to explore, just to cruise around sightseeing. I was taking pictures with my Treo cell phone to show Penny as we sped by famous landmarks.

Earl's cell phone rang so he pulled over to a nearby space by the curb he found and answered.

He listened for a bit then said, "Morry, I owe you big, thanks for that," and hung up.

"We have an appointment with someone who can fill us in on the mercenaries," he said as he pulled back out into traffic.

We drove for a bit, then he pulled into a parking lot by a building that had big letters on the side, "Federal Bureau of Investigation". I was wondering if Buck would come in with us, he said he was fine with the Feds; he just wasn't fond of Macomb County cops.

We went in to the reception desk and Earl said we were here to see Agent Wells. The woman behind the desk picked up her phone and called. She asked us to be seated and Agent Wells would be down shortly. Buck and Earl sat in the waiting area; I was walking around the lobby looking at the pictures on the walls of agents who were taken out in the line of duty. A big burly man came up and introduced himself as Art Wells, we introduced ourselves and he took us to his office up on the tenth floor.

On the way up in the elevator he spoke, "So you're friends with Morry Lang?"

Earl smiled and said, "We've known each other for about twenty years, we played together in numerous hotspots around the world."

Bob Moats

"I've known Morry for a bit less, he's one ornery cuss, and a man I wouldn't want mad at me." Wells looked at Earl and said, "Are you someone I should be afraid of too?"

"Not unless you're afraid of Detroit cops. I'm a pussycat now, no longer in service of the government. Now I'm just a cop out in Detroit, homicide and loving it." Earl responded.

"Detroit? You're a ways from your backyard?"

"Yeah, we came out here after a bust in Detroit led us to a connection to an organized crime outfit just starting up here. We're just advising here, helping to shut them down." Earl said.

"Well, Morry asked me to give you as much help as I can, let's see what we can do." He said as the elevator came to a halt and we exited. He led us down a long hallway and into his office. It was a newer building and had a lot of glass walls and chrome holding up everything. His desk was fancy with all kinds of computer devices spread out on it; I was envious.

"Ok, fill me in." Wells asked. Earl spent about a half hour giving all the info he could, short of saying anything about Marina's illegal status in this country. We hoped to keep that under wraps.

Wells was sitting back, then he reached over to his computer and was typing a bit, then he hit a button and a printer off the side of his desk sprang to life and shot out two pages of paper. He picked them up and studied a bit, then handed the papers to Earl. I was sitting next to Earl and he was holding it so I could see too. It was a short list of names and brief descriptions after each name of the men on the list and their involvement with mercenary dealings.

"You understand that this list is not open to the general public, but Morry vouches for you and since you are helping the local police to shut down Rex Erotica, I'm making this list available to you." He said it sounding a bit like a warning. "If you'll notice all names in bold are considered to be in the New York area and maybe available for work in the city. If Rex Erotica is hiring mercenaries, then these would be the ones to watch."

Earl said he was thankful for the help and asked if the FBI was watching Rex Erotica. Wells said that he had heard of the group, but they weren't big enough to worry about. Wells did ask about the kidnappings and interstate human trafficking, that was something the FBI would need to investigate.

"We had planned on sharing that info after we found out what Rex Erotica was up to, now we are better equipped to deal with the mess."

"I understand, but I'm going to send an agent over to talk to Brege about sticking our noses into it. Not way in, but just enough to keep us informed on the subject." He smiled.

"Right now our involvement in this whole thing is to find the missing girl and get her back home to Detroit safely." I said. "We're not interested in Rex Erotica other than helping with what we can to shut them down, so other girls aren't taken into their slime pit. This is something I have given my word to the girl's boyfriend and I intend to find her."

"Well, my office is open to help. If you need further assistance in finding your girl, I'll pull out the stops for you." Wells offered.

"Thanks, we may need it." I said. He handed me his card and said to call anytime.

We finished up, Wells took us back down to the street level, and we said our good-byes and went back to the car. Earl drove out as I was reading the list; it was a bit scary, what all these men were involved in. They were all located in the greater New York City area and I'm sure Brege could easily have men check them out.

We arrived back at Midtown Precinct and parked, then found Brege standing by the entrance door talking to another man. We came up and Brege introduced us to DA Mark Damon. Damon said with a smile that he heard of our exploits in the sleazy world of topless bars. Earl said it was all in the line of duty, someone had to do it.

Damon pulled us aside and said quietly, "We've had suspicions that certain officers in Vice have been looking the other way when it comes to Rex Erotica and their sex dealings. We are starting a quiet investigation into these allegations and we will find the men involved. Lieutenant Daws, anything you and your men find, please feel free to let me know."

Earl said he would love to take down dirty cops, we finished up and Damon left. Brege looked at Earl and said, "Didn't think when you drove out here you'd be in so much muck, eh Daws?"

Earl smiled and said he loved to play in the mud.

**

Chapter 21

Brege took us to his temporary office and then he sat looking over the list of mercenaries that Earl gave him. He thanked us for the list and called one of his men in to have him set up a task force to look into the men on the list, to see if they had any contact with

Rex Erotica. The detective went off and Brege turned back to us.

"I know you men came out here to find your missing girl and bring us the evidence that you found, but I appreciate any help you've given or can give. Earl, as a cop I'm sure you know how hard it is to keep track of criminals on the street. Here in New York we have ten times the trouble you got back in Detroit, and we are seriously understaffed. Any help is welcome, but I understand you have an agenda, that you men have things to do here besides get in deep shit with us." He looked sad as he said it.

I spoke, "Captain, we will do what we can to help bring down Rex Erotica. I'm sure I speak for Earl and Buck, we will help."

Earl and Buck both spoke their acknowledgments of support; Brege thanked us again.

"So what's the plan of attack?" Brege asked.

"Well, as you know my first priority is to find the missing girl, after that I'm available to perform for parties and Bar Mitzvahs." I joked.

Brege looked confused; Buck laughed and explained that I was a performing magician.

"Well, magic man, do your tricks to get us into Rex Erotica and take them down." Brege smiled.

Strip Club Murders

We finished wasting time and my cohorts and I left to go try Ladies Delight again. Driving over I was hoping that Marina didn't give them too much of a fight while they prepared her for the back rooms of their clubs. I was also hoping we could get in and out with her safely without violence. But being realistic, there would be trouble.

We arrived at the club and went in, greeted by the same dancer who took us to the back earlier, she laughed and said that we just couldn't stay away. I said we enjoyed the place and we were back for more. She took us to the door and got us in. I looked at the big no neck man guarding the door and figured Earl could take care of him. We went down the stairs into the main room and met a different madam this time; I hoped it wouldn't be a problem.

"Hello, what is your delight today?" She smiled.

"We were here last night and I asked the other woman in charge if you had any Russian girls working, she said there was a new girl but she wasn't due in till today. Is she in now?" I asked.

"Why yes, we have a fine young Russian girl in and waiting for you, or will your friends joining you?" She asked looking at Buck and Earl.

"Oh, no, they are just my bodyguards; I have many business dealings that necessitate the need to protect myself." I smiled. I thought I heard Earl snicker behind me.

"Well, your men can wait outside the door to your private room where the girl awaits you." She turned motioning me to follow. Earl whispered in my ear, next time he was the businessman and I was his valet. I looked at him and snorted.

We went down a long hallway and the madam stopped at a door and said to enjoy myself. I told my "bodyguards" to wait out here. They both suppressed a laugh and I went in the room.

The medium sized room was dark being lit only by a small lamp on a table by a queen-sized bed. The place did have class; the wallpaper was of a Victorian design half up the walls with an ornate lower wainscoting around the room. The bed had four brass post corners and the sheets were red silk. I could figure if I were paying for this, it would be an expensive ride. I looked around but saw no girl, then a door next to the bed opened and in she came, Marina, dressed in a silky black negligee, her make-up was garish and she walked like a zombie.

I wanted to yell for joy but I didn't want to frighten her or draw suspicion to myself. I walked to her and quietly said, "Marina, listen carefully, don't say anything, Ron sent me to bring you home."

Strip Club Murders

Her eyes were blank; she looked a bit drugged. She didn't respond when I mentioned Ron, I was a bit worried. I took hold of her shoulders and shook her a bit; she gave me a nasty look and then asked what I was doing.

"Are you Marina Koska?" I asked.

She looked at me hard, as if she wasn't quite sure what I was saying, but studying my words. She was definitely on something that was messing with her head. I took the picture of her and Ron from my pocket and held it up to her face. She looked at it and I could see a spark of recognition on her face, she then looked to me and had a strange look in her eyes.

"Ron? That's Ron. Oh, god, where is Ron?" she was panicking now. I had to hold her and whisper to her that Ron was fine and he was waiting for her back home in Detroit. She started weeping and I managed to reach for a tissue from a box on the bed stand.

"Marina, we have to get out of here, can you go with me and my friends. We will help you, but you have to want to get out." I said to her quietly.

She was rocking in my arms as I held her close. She looked up and I could see a little more life in her eyes. The emotions and adrenaline was flowing and she was fighting the drugs. I move back and told her to wait, I went to the door and opened it a crack and saw Buck standing by the door.

152

"Hey, is it clear out there?" I whispered. He looked to me and nodded his head. I said to get Earl and come in. Seconds later both men came into the room, Marina started to look panicky again; I went to her and told her they were friends who were going to help us get out. She moved close to me like I was her protector, I turned to Earl and said, "Should we call Brege and tell him we found the girl and he can take this place down?"

Earl looked like he was formulating something in his head and said, "Let's get her out of here first, and then bring in the troops. It would be safer that way, for her and us." He went to the door and looked out. I took my jacket off and told Marina to put it on covering her flimsy silk gown.

Earl looked out the door again and nodded to us. We came out the door just as the second madam came around a corner and saw us. She asked what we were doing, Earl held out his badge and said we were INS and this girl is in the country illegally and we were taking her to face deportation. The woman yelled, "Like hell you are." She pulled out a small device that looked like a garage door opener and pushed a button. We turned to go down the hall to the exit when a large man with a larger gun came out of a room blocking our way. He held up his gun to us and told us to back up.

Strip Club Murders

"You're messing with law enforcement, asswipe, want to go down hard?" Earl said as we stood in the middle of the hallway. Earl was partially behind me, blocked enough so he could take his gun out of its holster. Buck saw this and did the same. Earl started to move away from me going to the left of the hall and then Buck got the idea and moved right. By now they each had their guns at their sides where the big man could see.

"Okay, Brainiac, You're thinking, you can take out one of us, but will you be fast enough to get the other before he shoots your big ass?" Earl taunted.

The big man was starting to sweat and his gun hand was going back and forth between Earl and Buck, but he wasn't watching me as I took out my Glock behind Marina.

I heard a movement behind me and turned my head to see the madam coming with a shotgun, I pushed Marina down and spun, firing my Glock at her, then all hell broke loose. Earl and Buck both fired on the big man, as the madam fell back from the wound in her shoulder where the shotgun formerly rested. Earl looked over and said good shooting, then asked why I didn't plug her good. I smiled as I helped up Marina and said that I was aiming for her head.

"Never go for the small of the head, always for the body, more landscape to hit." Earl smiled.

I said, "I'll remember that next time I have to shoot a madam carrying a shotgun."

**

Chapter 22

We heard noises on the stairs coming from the club; I said to follow me as we went through a door into a one of the sex rooms, disturbing a very obese, excessively hairy, bald-headed man getting it on with some redhead. You could barely see her under him, I stopped and looked at them and said, "That's disgusting." I led everyone to the door next to the bed, same as the one Marina came through in her room. I figured there must be a back way to dressing rooms or something, I didn't really have any idea where it led, just hoped it took us out.

I was partially right as it came out to a narrow hallway and I had no idea which way to go. Marina spoke, "Go right, it leads to the room where we clean up and there is a door going outside, but there is also another man guarding it."

I nodded at Earl and we went that way, coming to what looked like a locker room. There was no one in the room, I figured the guard heard the shooting and went to see what was going on. We ran to the door as Marina pointed to it. We just got to it as gunshots rang out and bullets whizzed by us. Earl and Buck spun returning shots at the man as he stood by the corner of a second hallway. He dropped, and I pushed on the door, it exited into a stairway going up, which we went. The door at the top of the stairs opened into the dressing room of the stripper in the club. They saw us coming through with guns drawn and started screaming.

Just as we thought we were getting away, about four men came streaming into the room and when they finally saw us, started shooting. We returned fire as we tried to hide behind lockers and tables, they doing the same. It was an old fashion western gun battle, but this was real and so were the bullets. I had Marina down behind a dressing table that had a full back to it and yelled to Earl, "Think we should have called Brege?" He smiled at me and said, "Hey, we got it under control. Brege can come in and clean-up after us."

I fired only when necessary to conserve ammo, since I didn't have another clip, the thugs were shooting like crazy. I yelled to Earl again, "This is not a movie, when do they run out of bullets?" Soon, he said by the way they are wasting ammo. Earl went around the lockers he was hiding behind, and I couldn't see him anymore, then I heard a barrage of gunfire. After a minute things got quiet, I peeked around and Earl was standing out by the bodies of two of the men. I stood slowly and saw Buck kicking at a body off his side of the room.

Earl yelled, "Let's get the hell out before they call for real reinforcements." We went for the door leading to the club and went down the main aisle with our guns still out, but hidden by our side, so not to alarm the men engrossed in the strippers. We hit the outer front door and on to the street, just as cop cars were streaming down the street out front. We turned and went around the building before they could get to us. We were in the Charger and Marina was in back safely with Buck. I looked at Earl and said, "You gonna call Brege now to explain the mess we just left in there?" He agreed it was time to confess and took out his cell and called Brege.

Brege told us to come in to fill out our reports on the ruckus and get our asses covered. We drove back to Midtown and went into Brege's office space. I introduced Marina and Brege asked if she was well enough to give a statement on her ordeal? She was still a bit woozy and confused, plus she was more afraid the police would send her back to Russia, I said personally to her not to say anything about that. They gave her some coveralls from janitorial to wear, so I could put my jacket back on covering my Glock.

I asked Brege to talk off the side and he came with me until we were away from everyone. "Captain, I need to explain a few things, I hope I can trust in your discretion and make an offer. Can we talk candidly?"

He looked at me, gave a slight nod of his head and said to speak.

"Marina is not a citizen of the U.S.; she was smuggled here by way of an agent of our own government from Russia to escape prostitution and bondage there by the Russian Mafia. She started working in Detroit while studying towards getting citizenship. Unfortunately, she was kidnapped by Rex Erotica and forced into prostitution here. She's had bad breaks for way too long. If she goes back to Russia, she may die, she wants to stay here and I intend to see she does. You need her testimony to put Rex Erotica out of business for kidnapping and prostitution. Slavery is in there somewhere, I'm sure, so if she agrees to testify, is there some way we can help her to stay here?"

Brege smiled and said, "You get real close to your work don't you?"

"I care for the people I'm asked to protect or find, yes."

"I'll talk to a few people I know in INS and see what we can do, I'll do my best. Now let's get her statement and shut the fuckers down."

"You got it." We shook on it and went back to Marina. I asked if I could talk to her alone for a minute and we went off to an office Brege pointed us to. We went in and I told Marina to sit.

"Marina, Ron sent me to find you, it wasn't easy and you have been through an ordeal. Now we need you to help stop the men who kidnapped you and send them to prison. Can you do that?" I asked.

She nodded and I took out my cell phone and hit speed dial for Ron. After about four rings, he came on and I told him it was me and had someone who wanted to talk to him. I put on Marina and she said hello, then she broke down and cried when he went crazy on the other end. They talked for a good minute and she told him she was well now. I said she could talk more later and took the phone. "Ron, she's okay, I'm going to watch her for you, she needs to testify against the men who took her now, I'll let her talk to you more later tonight, when we are more rested. Take care and be patient." We finished and I hung up. I looked to Marina and said let's go nail the slime merchants.

We went back out to the rest of our crew, I sat Marina in a chair next to Brege's desk, and he sat telling her that she would be all right.

Brege had a woman in from court reporting to take her statement and the DA came in to witness the testimony. Marina started from when she was kidnapped in Detroit, telling where she was taken and then her trip out to New York. She told of the building the four girls were taken to and the beatings they got and drugs they were forced to take. She said she wasn't even sure where she was after a while; she was so messed up. She told the DA about things she heard earlier in the room they were kept, how the men were deciding on who would stay in New York and who would go to Hong Kong and who would be sold to the clients who wanted sex slaves. She didn't know how they operated, but heard what they said through the walls.

Brege's phone rang and he answered, listened and then hung up. He called me, Earl and Buck to the side.

"Good news and bad; good news is they got Ladies Delight under control and closed up for now, bad news is Rex Erotica somehow got the hookers out of the club, but there were a few that didn't make it. They were killed, about four of them, executed. Guess Rex Erotica didn't want anyone testifying against them. These people are ruthless bastards. You have to protect Marina the best you can, she's all we got now. I'll give you a few men to help you if you want. Let me know." He went back to his office to watch the rest of Marina's testimony.

I looked to Earl and Buck and said, "We have a lot to do now. We can take Marina back to Detroit and forget the whole thing or let Marina testify, putting these SOB's away and we pull double duty protecting her. Anyone want to go home?"

Buck said he was having fun here in New York and Earl said he had nothing better to do. I smiled and said, "Let's rock and roll."

**

Chapter 23

We took Marina back to our room and I knew I had to give up the big bed. I called room service and asked them to bring up another rollaway bed and they took care of it.

I called Penny around 9 P.M. and she came on sounding better. "How's my little girl?"

"Horny, and you're not here, what gives?"

"Hey, I got my missing girl, at least be happy for that." I defended myself.

"Sweetie, I'm very happy you found her. Now are you coming home, I said I was horny."

I laughed, "I'm sorry, but we have to take care of a few more details here. Shouldn't take too long. How are you feeling by the way?" I said trying to divert the answer I gave about having to stay longer.

"You're stalling on my question about when you're coming home, when?" She didn't miss a trick.

"Well, Marina is testifying about her ordeal with the crime syndicate and we have to protect her till she does. Maybe a few days, can't tell right now." I said weakly.

"Okay, there goes your sex for a month."

"Hey don't punish me, besides, if you put me off for a month that means you are put off too."

She was quiet for a beat and then said, "Okay, that's true, I'll have to think of a better punishment for you when you get home."

We talked for a while longer then I said I had to let Marina talk to Ron and I would call her again tomorrow.

I took Marina to the bedroom, dialed Ron, and gave the phone to her. She started crying again and I went out of the room to let them talk. Earl and Buck were sitting watching TV and I called room service and ordered up some beer, sprite, and snacks.

Marina finished with her call, came out of the bedroom and I offered her a beer, she took it. She sat and thanked us again for getting her out of that place. I said it was all in a day's work and we had more important things to take care of now, like putting away the bad guys. She said they were very bad to her and she hoped they'd fry in hell. I was just now noticing her Russian accent and told her I knew a few words in Russian, I said them and she giggled out loud.

"Did I say it right? I was told it meant, 'Hello comrade how are you', that's what I was taught." I offered.

She laughed and said, "You said 'Hello chicken, are you good', and that's not bad if you wanted to say that."

Everyone laughed and we watched TV and made small talk. I asked Marina about Russia and if she missed it. She said she did very much, but not the poverty and crime that was getting worse now since the Soviet Union had broken up. She loved the United States and hoped she could stay. I said we had a number of people who would help with that. Earl spoke up and said he could blackmail a number of government officials into making her a citizen. I looked at him and believed he could, it was something to remember.

It was getting late and Marina looked droopy, so I said we should call it a night. She started off to the bedroom, I said I was sorry we didn't have any bed clothing she could wear, she said that was all right, she slept in the nude anyways. I had to stop my mind from thinking what it was, I just kept thinking of Penny naked and spread out on our bed. Marina was a very attractive woman, slim build, on the tall side, about five-ten, and very long blond hair, almost down to her waist. She had strikingly blue eyes; I figured she had a bit of Swede in her. I had to think hard on Penny now as Marina went off to the bedroom, closing the door.

I pulled out the rollaway bed and had to put it by the front door because Earl and Buck had spread out around the room. We all laid down and I reached up, killed the light switch, and tried to sleep. I knew I wouldn't go to sleep right away so laid there thinking about the day. I was thinking about the poor women who were forced into hooking and then executed, taking away their lives. So sad. I started to doze off; I guess I was more tired than I thought.

I don't know when it happened, I couldn't see a clock, but I heard a noise at the door. I was a light sleeper when it came to noises I didn't like, so I laid listening as it sounded like a key was in the door, or someone jimmying the lock. I rolled out of the day bed and crawled to Earl since he was the closest to me. I shook him and he came up with his gun in my face. I backed off and quietly said to save it for whoever is trying to get in the room. He rolled off his bed and threw a pillow at Buck, he came up ready to fight and I quietly yelled to him to be quiet. He looked at the two of us on the floor, figured something was wrong, and had his .38 up and ready. I took my Glock from under my pillow and Earl had already crawled to the side of the door and sat listening. We could hear the lock being picked and then the knob turned slowly and the door opened a crack.

Whoever was on the other side was listening to the room and then the door opened more. The figure was shadowed by the light in the hallway and then another figure came up behind the first. Earl was on one side of the door and I was between a desk and the door on the other side. The figures came in slowly and past us as I reached up and flicked on the light. Earl had his gun stuck in the neck of one of the men, Buck had his .38 on the nose of the other and I came around pointing my gun at both. The men froze and Earl yelled for them to put hands on their head as he patted them down and taking their guns and putting them in his belt. Then he told them to get down on their knees or he would start shooting kneecaps. They did. Earl went for his handcuffs and cuffed both their right wrists together, saying to me if they try to running they'll be stumbling over each other. It made sense to me.

We pulled them both up and Earl got in their faces, "Rex Erotica sent you didn't they?"

They said nothing, Earl said, "I don't care for scum like you, I've done away with a lot of scum in my days with the CIA. I'm giving you a chance to talk or

Strip Club Murders

I'll make you wish you were being detained by Homeland Security and their torture."

One of the men looked a bit shocked and he was squirming. Earl went to his gym bag and took out a pair of pliers. I wondered why he was carrying those, but didn't ask. He waved the pliers in front of the man who had squirmed and said, "Give me your left hand."

The man looked terrified and said, "You can't do that to us, you're a cop and you can't do that!"

"I'm a cop in Detroit and you're about to find out what we do to scumballs in Detroit." He laughed evilly, grabbed the man's left hand, and started to attach the pliers to the man's fingers. He screamed before Earl even started to squeeze his finger. I was trying not to laugh and Buck had turned away to hide his face as he laughed.

The man was trying to pull away and he said to stop, he'd talk. The other man told him to shut his mouth, and then Earl whacked the mouthy man with his gun causing the man to drop to the floor pulling the second man down. The second man looked up and said he'd still talk; just don't hurt him. Earl got down close to the man and said to speak. The man said they were sent by some guy who hired them to whack some Russian bitch who could finger too many people. He didn't know who it was that hired him;

they just got the information by phone and came here to do the hit.

I was thinking this guy was a lousy hit man; he was probably wetting his pants about now. Earl stood and said to watch them and went to get his cell phone and called Brege. It was just now after 2 A.M. but Brege answered and Earl told him what we had. Brege said he'd have some men come to get the perps and then he'd station a couple uniforms outside our door. Earl said that would work and hung up.

He got up close to the men and said their ride would be along shortly.

**

Chapter 24

By 3:30 A.M., our room was back to normal. There were two cops outside our door and I took out two of the room's chairs for them to sit on, along with a small table and a deck of cards the room provided. I guess the hotel thought their guests had nothing better to do than play cards. Marina was still asleep in the bedroom, I wanted to look in to see if she was all right, but I was afraid she'd be uncovered and I didn't really want to see her naked, well I did, but it wouldn't be right. I listened at the door and I could hear her snoring lightly, so I knew she was all right.

I sat on my day bed and said to Buck and Earl, "This is looking serious, I'm not fond of having hit men coming after us, even lousy ones. We need a plan."

"I think first, we should move to another hotel or at least another room. Who all knew where we were staying here?" Buck asked.

Earl said, "Brege had that info, and anyone in the precinct could have gotten to it. I'm wondering about vice right now, Damon, the DA, said he felt they were in on the dealings of Rex Erotica's whorehouses. Maybe they heard we managed to get one witness out and they warned Rex Erotica about her. They could have easily gotten our location and sent someone to eliminate their problem."

"Crap, now we have to worry about the crime lords and the cops. This is getting bad. We need to put her in deep cover till they can get this settled, someplace safe." I sat and thought for a bit then looked at Buck, "Buck, you remember Angelo from Vegas?" He nodded and said he did, I continued, "I have an idea, may not work but it's worth the try. It's too late to call now, have to wait until morning. On that note, I'm going to try and get back to sleep."

We all agreed on that and with the police outside our door, I felt safe enough to sleep again. Amazingly, I did go to sleep, I guess I was more tired than worried. Morning came and I awoke to find Marina sitting on the couch facing me. She gave me a smile that had me sitting up and ready to go.

She said something in Russian then apologized, "Sorry, I forgot you only talk Russian to chickens." She laughed and said she wished me a good morning. I asked her to repeat it and I tried to say it a few times. I suddenly heard Earl speaking from his bed, it sounded like Russian and Marina clapped her hands and laughed.

"Okay, he said something bad about me, didn't he?" I asked Marina.

"He said you were the chicken." She said slyly.

Earl got up and swung his feet over the side of the day bed, said something again in Russian and went into the bathroom. I looked to Marina and she said, "He said to ask chicken boy if he could order coffee for him. I don't think of you as a chicken."

"I'm more of a turkey boy sometimes, but never a chicken." I smiled.

Buck started to stir and then brought his body up in the bed, like a zombie rising from a grave, slowly and clawing at the air. He stretched and yawn loudly. He looked over to us and said good morning. Marina and I both said good morning to him in Russian. He looked perplexed and said, "Is my hearing messed up?"

Earl came out of the bathroom and said not to go in there for a few minutes, then asked where his coffee was. I looked at Marina and asked if she would like breakfast, she said, please, she would. I knew Buck would take whatever I got, so I stood and went to the phone and called Room Service, after looking out in the hall and asking the cops if they'd like breakfast, they accepted. Room Service had the food and coffee to our room by the time we all had ourselves dressed and ready to eat. Earl took his pot of coffee to the desk and sat back savoring the aroma of the coffee.

After my breakfast, I went to the bedroom, took my cell phone out and called Angelo's private number he gave me when he first called about the case. I waited, and then he came on. I told him it was me and he asked how I was doing, then I gave him a brief rundown of our adventures here in New York and told him about finding Ron's girl and the danger she was in right now. Okay, I did build it up a bit, but I wanted to make a point. I asked for a big favor from him, for his cousin, and me he said to name it, he would be pleased to do it. I said I wanted to put Marina somewhere she would be really safe, I asked if he knew a place where we could do that. He didn't even hesitate and said to bring her to the family compound, he'd talk to Francis and he was sure she would help out. He gave me the address and I said we'd be there by noon. He said that was good, to give him time to arrange with the staff for a place for her. I thanked him and said we'd be there.

I went back out, pulled Buck and Earl away from Marina, and told them of my plan. Earl gave me a surprised look and said, "You're going to hide a key witness with the mob, that's different. Rex Erotica would never dare to think to attack her there."

"Earl, don't take offense, but I'm going to take Marina over with Buck and I think you look a bit too much like a cop to take into the mob household, at least for this first time. Angelo knows Buck so it would be easier that way."

"I take no offense; I would prefer to stay away from the mob, so I'll go bother Brege. I won't tell him what you're planning, just that you are hiding her until she's needed. I'm going to talk to him about the possible leak on our location, see if we can come up with someone who nosed around for the address. Maybe we'll catch a dirty cop or two."

We all agreed on our plans and I went out to see Marina. I looked at her and she had a blanket wrapped around her, I forgot she came with no clothes, other than the janitor coveralls, that were presentable to wear on the street. I got her the long overcoat I brought, then Buck and Earl joined me in taking her down to the lobby stores, and there we bought her some jeans, shirts and a nice jacket. I told the cops they could use the room while we were gone and we'd be back shortly.

Marina was pleased with the clothes and she looked good in them. She was half my age, and if I weren't with Penny, I wouldn't mind it if Marina like much older men. I had to get my mind back on track, I'm sure Penny is back in Michigan with an alarm in her head going off, saying Jim is cheating on me. We went back to the elevators and up to our floor, the doors slid opened and we went out into the hallway.

Earl held up his hand and we stopped. He was sniffing and I did too. It's smelled like gunpowder. Earl told us to wait and he walked down the hall with his weapon drawn. Our room door burst open and Earl brought up his gun and stopped. It was one of the cops; he was bleeding from his shoulder and said they were jumped. He said it was safe now, he and his partner shot the attackers and he had already called reinforcements. Earl looked back at us and said to me, "You better get her to your friends quickly, this is escalating."

"I'm surprised they would try something so soon after the last attempt." I said as all the cops were taking care of the new crime scene. Brege was watching the proceedings.

"They figured we would let down our guard. So hit again before the iron cools," Brege offered.

"Captain, I'm taking Marina somewhere she will be absolutely safe but I'm not saying, there are moles in the department and I don't want anyone knowing. So if you'll excuse us we have an appointment to keep." I saluted the Captain and Earl, and then Buck and I took Marina out. The Captain yelled, asking if we needed a police escort, I yelled back that was the last thing I wanted right now. The elevator door closed and Buck and I went down to the lobby.

Earl looked at the Captain and said that when we had gone shopping the hitmen evidently didn't know we had left. They knocked at the door saying they were picking up our breakfast cart. They must have seen it going in, but missed us going out. Our luck. The one cop opened the door and the hitman shot him, luckily in the shoulder. The other cop drew and took out the first hitman and even though the other cop was hit, it wasn't his gun arm, he drew from the floor and took out the second hitman."

"Damn I want this to end; Rex Erotica is going too far. This morning I put warrants out for everyone involved and we are rounding up most of them, but the big boss, McKinley and his henchmen are still at large, hiding out by now I imagine. We will find them."

"I hope we can do some checking and find out who in the department is feeding the bad guys with the info on Marina. Shall we put our heads together and track them down?" Earl smiled. Brege said let's go.

Chapter 25

Buck and I went to the car rental counter of the hotel and rented a car, this time a small one to be speedy around the crazy traffic in New York. After our car was brought around, we got in and drove off to the side of the road. I asked Buck if he saw anyone watching us, he said he was looking and saw no one. I pulled out my Palm TX and did a search on the address Angelo gave me, it came up and we headed up Manhattan taking a few detours around the area and backtracking so hopefully to lose a tail.

We hit the Interstate 85 and went north towards a town called Dobbs Ferry. It was a small community on the Hudson River, quiet town, not knowing they had a mob family ensconced in their midst, or maybe they do. After a forty-minute drive, we found the walled fortress that housed the Traviano family compound. We drove up to the gate to where there was one of those intercoms that you would announce your arrival. I pushed the button and waited, a minute later a voice asked what we wanted. I said that Angelo DeMarco was expecting us. The gates swung slowly open and I drove up the long, well-landscaped drive to the circular drive at the front entrance. We pulled up and everyone got out of the car. I stood looking at the huge well-manicured lawn and expertly trimmed hedges. There was money here, just in landscaping costs and I'm sure there were staff running the place, Francis would never have to do a dish here.

Angelo came busting out the front door and gave me a bear hug that just about made me breathless. Angelo showed me he still had the Rolex watch I gave him in Vegas. He shook Buck's hand and said he remembered him from Vegas. Buck said it was a pleasure to see him again. I introduced Marina to Angelo and he gave her a hug, more carefully this time and said it was good to finally meet Ron's girlfriend. Marina gave the big man a kiss on the cheek and Angelo actually blushed. He said for us to come in and we found ourselves in a big foyer, then he took us down a long hallway to a room off the side, it was a large library-like room.

Angelo asked us to sit and he would be right back, he left the room and we just sat in awe of the place. The room had dozens of antique objects and oil paintings on every wall between the stacks of books, tons of them all around the room. There was a very ornately carved desk at the side of the room, with a huge desk chair of carved wood and red satin cushioning. It was a room I could live in.

Strip Club Murders

Buck gave a low chuckle and said he couldn't believe he was actually in a mob capo's house. I said to be easy on the mob capo reference; he nodded and went to look out the window. He said there was water behind them; I said that was probably the Hudson River. Nice place, on the river too.

After a couple of minutes, Angelo returned and he had a friendly face with him, Francis Traviano. We stood and I said, "Mrs. Traviano, I want to thank you for your kind offer to help with our little problem."

Francis went right to Marina and said, "Angelo explained your situation and it isn't a little problem. Marina you are welcome in our house and under our protection. Angelo will be your personal bodyguard while you are here." It was like meeting the Queen of England; she was so regal in her bearing and poise. I didn't know, but estimated her age to be around her middle to late seventies. She had her black-gray hair up on a bun and she wore a floor length dress that reminded me of what women wore in medieval days. She came to me and asked, "Is Penny and that cute little pup with you, I watch her show almost every day now."

"I'm sorry, but she and Willy are back in Michigan, Penny came down with a bug and wasn't up to traveling, besides this trip is a little too dangerous to involve her." I replied.

"I understand, hopefully you can come back again another time under less dangerous circumstances and bring her." She smiled.

"Yes, I will and I'm sure she would love to do a show on you someday. How you stayed on top of things for so long." I said hoping it didn't offend.

Her eyes grew and she said she'd absolutely love that. She asked us to all sit and we did.

She sat in a high back chair that looked like it came out of a cathedral, one a bishop would sit on, she looked good in the chair. She asked me to explain what brought us to this day and I started back when Angelo first called me about Ron's problem. About a half later, I finished and she smiled.

"Jim, I'm sure you know what I am and my connections to the life. My Gino would never condone drugs, prostitution or slavery, it's vulgar and hooking is demeaning to women. Yes, what we do is not so legal either, but everyone must have an occupation, we just have one that goes back centuries to my country of Italy. It's hard to get out of the family business, if you know what I mean." She gave us a big smile.

The library door opened again and in walked don Gino Traviano himself. I remembered him from their wedding in Vegas, although in Vegas I thought he was at least 100 years old, he looked much younger now, marriage must have agreed with him. Francis stood and went to him, saying these are the people she told him about. He smiled widely and said his house was ours, welcome. He came to me and was shaking my hand and saying he saw Penny's show that I was on talking about the Bridezilla killer. He winked and thanked me for the kind words about his wedding and mostly for helping to save his Franny when she was taken by the Bridezilla killer. I thought his reference to Francis as Franny was cute.

He said to sit, he wasn't formal. We did.

"Jimmy, tell me about your problem." He asked. I re-ran the story again and he was nodding all through it. I finished and he was quiet, and then spoke, "I have been watching this Rex Erotica for some time, since they started buying those strip clubs in the city. I had my people closely on their movements; I wasn't going to interfere unless they messed with my business connections, so I looked the other way. But now they have interfered with family, Angelo is Franny's son and his cousin Ron is part of her family so that makes Marina part of our family too. No one messes with family. Marina you will feel safe with us and when you testify against Rex Erotica, our presence will be felt. Jimmy you said you were attacked by four hit men?"

I was taken aback by his statement that Angelo was Francis' son; I didn't know that. "Yes sir, they weren't the best hitmen they could have sent, we captured the first two and the second two were killed by the police who were protecting us."

"Jimmy, you don't have to call me sir, it's Gino to you and your friends, and I treat you like family now. I'll have someone check on these hitmen to see where they came out of. Get some names to Angelo, he can run them down for you."

"That would be helpful for the police." I said.

Gino smiled and said, "I remember when we used to handle these things in our own way, now days it's so complicated. We'll do this the new way. Don't worry about a thing." He stood and said he had work to do out in the garden. He came to Marina and said, "My child, you are welcome here anytime." Marina asked him what kind of garden he had; he said his flower garden, why? Marina asked if she could help him, she loved working with flowers. He looked to Francis and asked if she trusted him with such a good-looking woman, she laughed and told Marina not to give him a heart attack. Gino helped Marina up and they went out.

I said to Francis, "I didn't know Angelo was your son." Angelo was sitting back in his chair smiling.

Francis looked at Angelo and said he was her son by her first marriage. Angelo's father was the head of the New York DeMarco family, but he was knocked off and that family split up, then later she married Carlo

Mangelo from New Jersey. He died of undetermined causes, and then along came Gino. Now he'll be showing off for Marina out in the garden, exerting himself and will probably die of heart failure, she laughed.

**

Chapter 26

Francis excused herself to go make sure Gino was behaving himself and left Angelo, Buck and I alone in the room. I told Angelo I was going to call in for the hitmen's names and he said to go ahead. I got on my cell phone and called Earl, after three rings he came on.

"Hey chicken boy, what's up?" He laughed.

"Okay, that's not funny anymore, besides I have the Traviano family on my side, so unless you want problems, knock it off." I grinned.

He said he was done and asked what I needed. "I want all the names of the hitmen who visited us this morning; you got it handy, Sherlock?" I heard him asked Brege if he had the perps names on hand and there was a pause, then he came back. "Ready, I got them." Earl rattled off the names of the men as I wrote them down. He finished and I said to go back to hunting down dirty cops. I looked at the list and handed it to Angelo, he smiled and said he'd have it checked out and put the list in his pocket, then asking if we would like a tour of the estate. I was having chills to be able to go around the place, so Buck and I followed Angelo out as he started to take us around the house. We eventually came to a room that was filled with computers and he excused himself for a minute and went in. We could still see him as he went to a man at a one of the many consoles and handed him the paper of names. He came back out to us and said now days a good business has to be up on technology.

We went outside and he showed us the grounds including stables and a huge garage with about ten classic cars. Buck was excited to see all the beautifully kept up cars. We went out and around to the back of the house and found Francis sitting on a lawn chair by the huge flower beds watching Gino and Marina enjoying themselves weeding, culling the flowers and planting new ones. Francis told us to pull up some chairs and sit, we did. I was looking around the property and I could see surveillance cameras and there were a number of huge men walking around the grounds, they had assault weapons. Angelo saw me watching them and commented that they were just the one we could see, there was more protection that would surprise me.

Strip Club Murders

Francis smiled and said, "I love this place, so peaceful, Gino loves flowers and I love Gino. I know he's older than I am and may go before me, but I will have good memories of our time together. He is a good man despite his occupation; he takes care of me and loves me. Yes Jim, we still do have a good sex life." Something I really didn't need to hear, but thought about my relationship with Penny and our sex life. We probably would do it until our bones were too brittle to attempt it anymore. "Do you and Penny still have a good, healthy sex life?" She caught me off guard with that question.

"Well, amazingly we do. She's quite a woman and extremely horny, I can say that because she would admit to it also." I smiled.

She laughed a nice easy laugh, "Yes, being horny does help, and I've seen Penny on her show, she looks like she can handle it." Francis looked back at Gino and laughed when he slipped in the mulch and fell on his rear. I was a bit worried he might hurt himself, Francis could see my concern and said not to worry, Gino was strong as an ox, and he won't break.

As we sat watching Gino, a man came out from the house, gave Angelo a paper, and walked back to the house. Angelo looked at the paper and I could hear him say crap under his breath.

182

I asked him what was wrong. He looked at me and said the hitmen were indeed mercenaries that were brought in from Jersey and they had more following if needed. He asked me to be careful going back to our hotel room, have lots of protection. He asked if I wanted a few of his men to come along, I said that I appreciated his offer, but to hold that thought and I would let him know later if we need back up.

I commented on how poorly the first four hitmen operated, he was looking at the list and said they were getting worse. He handed me the paper and I looked at it. There were names and descriptions of about eight men that had been hired through a network of mercenaries and they had more coming as needed. I said to Angelo that we should be heading back to the big city and thanked Francis again for her hospitality, I yelled to Gino that we had to leave, he waved and said we better come back to visit or he'd send someone out to get us. I laughed, but thought that sounded like a threat. I knew we'd have to come back to get Marina, so we'd keep the old man happy. Marina ran over, gave Buck and me a kiss on the cheek, and said to be careful. Buck and I left, getting back to our car and headed south to the Midtown precinct, I let Buck drive. I called Earl, asked for Brege, and read off the info we got about the hitmen and where they came from. I said we'd be there in about a half hour and we could go from there.

We arrived at Midtown and had to park down the street, we didn't have the privilege of being a cop car to park in front of the building. We went in and got to Brege's office and I was very surprised to see Ron sitting by Brege's cubicle. He smiled and stood, coming over to us.

"I couldn't wait to see Marina and I was worried for her safety, so I came out. I called Earl since he gave me his card long ago when he was looking into that murder by my club. He told me where he was and I grabbed a cab here. Earl says you guys have hidden Marina so the bad guys can't get to her." He looked excited to meet up again with his girlfriend.

"Yep, we have her hidden so well; no one can get to her, unless they are crazy." I smiled. "Let me arrange transportation for you." I said as I pulled out my cell phone and dialed Angelo. He came on and I explained that Ron was with me and wanted to see Marina. Angelo was happy to hear his cousin was in town, he hadn't seen him in years, and his Aunt Francis would love to see him. He said he would send a car to pick him up and I told him where we were; he told me were they would pick him up at.

"Ron, we are dealing with some pretty connected men, do not under any circumstances tell anyone where you are going, no one, understood?" I warned him.

"I won't tell a soul; Marina has already had enough troubles." He said.

Earl came over and said, "I'm imagining that you're arranging for Ron to be taken out to where you stashed Marina. Did you have cooperation with the people where you took her?"

"They are actually very nice people. I was more welcome there, than with my own relations." I grinned.

Earl looked at me and then finally smiled, "Well she is really safe there." He turned to Ron, "I'm sure Jim warned you not to say where you are going?"

"He did, I just want to be with Marina, I don't care where she is." Ron said.

I offered, "I'm sure you'll be happy where you are going. Now we will drive you to where you are going to be picked up." I told Earl that we would be back shortly.

I took Ron and Buck back out to our car and I saw someone lurking around the car. We got closer and I yelled startling the man, who looked up, then ran. Buck was in better health than I was and he took chase, managing to nail the guy before he could get too far. I ran up with my Glock out and called Earl. A few minutes later, Earl and Brege came up with three uniforms. In the time they took to get there, I tried to question him but he wasn't very cooperative. Buck went to look at the car and he dropped to the ground and saw the device attached to the undercarriage, unconnected wires still hanging down. We stopped him before he could complete his mission. Brege called for the bomb squad and they came to remove the device.

"How the hell did they know what car we had?" I was mad now.

"They must have watched you rent the car and then waited for you to be away from the vehicle to plant the bomb." Earl surmised.

I said quietly to Earl, "They must not have followed us to the Traviano property; they definitely wouldn't have messed with us then."

He smiled and said, "We may need the family's help eventually. It couldn't hurt."

**

Chapter 27

I looked to Brege and asked if they had McKinley in custody yet? He said they were still working on it. My cell phone rang and it was Angelo saying that they were at the pickup point and asked where we were. I told him what just happened and we'd be there shortly. I told Earl and Brege that we had to go and we'd be back later.

We drove out to a Starbucks that Angelo told us to go to and I saw the long black Lincoln Town Car parked in the lot. We drove up and Angelo stepped out the passenger door, Ron made a happy noise and jumped out of our rental. The two big men hugged and slapped at each other, as I sat looking at them thinking we needed more joy in our lives. Angelo came over and said he wasn't happy about a bomb attempt to hurt us, he again offered to have his men watch over us, I thanked him again and said we may need his offer later. He thanked me for bringing Ron out and said to be sure to stop out for a visit even before we needed Marina.

Buck and I drove back to Midtown and in to where we started at. Earl was standing outside an interview room and saw us, he waved and we went into the observation room. The guy who tried to attach the bomb to our rental was sitting alone at the table. Earl asked Brege if he could be in on the interview and we were waiting for a rep from the DA's office. I asked Earl if they interviewed the two thugs we captured this morning, Earl said they attempted to, but they both lawyered up.

"Probably figuring McKinley will get them off with his team of high priced lawyers." I said.

Strip Club Murders

The ADA finally arrived and Earl said show time. Brege met him in the hall and they went in. Brege sat across from the guy and Earl went and stood behind him. The guy was looking in the mirror at Earl and had a worried expression. Earl just stood leaning against the wall and smirking at the guy.

"We tracked your prints down, your name is Sylvester Knox, is that correct?" Brege asked.

The man was silent, then Earl snapped his ear lightly and the man yelped. "Hey, that's police brutality!" He yelled. Earl leaned in close to his ear and said somewhat quietly, but I could hear him, "You want to see real police brutality, I'm not a cop here, I'm a cop in Detroit and we are nice and brutal to scum like you. I'm here to make sure that you talk real nice to the Captain. Do you read me snotbucket?"

The man had a perplexed look on his face and asked, "You're from Detroit?" Earl acknowledged him. He sat a bit longer and then Earl snapped him on the ear again. He flinched and Earl said that's just the start.

Brege asked again, "You're name is Sylvester Knox?"

The man nodded, Brege said this interview is being video recorded unless he object to it. Earl coughed loudly; the man jumped and said it would be fine with him. He then said he was Sly Knox.

"Ok, let's see how sly you are. You were apprehended in the process of planting an explosive device under a car this afternoon, correct?" Brege asked.

The man was silent again, Earl hummed the death theme, and the man went wide-eyed and said he was.

"Who hired you to set up the kill?"

Now he looked really panicky, "Oh, hell man, if I tell you that, he'll kill me."

"Who will kill you?"

"The guy who hired me, he'll do it."

"Who will do it?"

"The guy."

Earl grabbed Sly's hair and pulled him back, "You tell us his name and we'll protect you, otherwise, we'll turn you loose and start a rumor that you ratted out everyone in your little mercenary group."

Sly's face took on a new meaning to fear, "You really think you can protect me?"

"Well, we've stopped five attempts on the life of our witness just today, we can protect you." Earl offered and let his hair go. He leaned forward on the table and looked at Brege and said quietly, "His name is Edward Franks; he's the organizer for the 102nd Militia out of Jersey. He sets up all the local assignments in New York for our men, hits for hire he calls it. Eliminates the need to keep men on a payroll like the mob does."

Earl came around and stood next to Brege, "Where can we find this Franks?"

"Hell, I don't know, he's hiding out in the city somewhere and just hires us by phone, then we find our pay in the mail, no return address.

Earl looked to Brege and said, "I'll get hold of my contact and see what they have on him. I only needed a name, thanks, doofus." He said to Sly and left the room. Brege called for a uniform to take Sly back to his cell. He walked out of the room.

Buck and I left the observation room, went with Brege to his desk, and asked, "What's going on with the strip clubs?"

"We've shut down all ten that Rex Erotica own here, and arrested a few of the employees working the prostitution angle, but they are all too afraid to rat. We just need to get McKinley and his lieutenants to make it a full boat. I got my men working the slavery angle, we found a number of financial transactions from foreign sources in their offices and we're running them down. After we get Marina to testify on the kidnapping and forced prostitution, they'll all go down easier. I presume your girl is tucked away safely."

"Oh, yeah, a place so safe Rex Erotica would never dare to go after her." I smiled.

As Buck and I stood by his desk, one of his detectives came rushing up and said they found McKinley. He's holed up in a high-rise apartment in East Village across from Tompkins Square; he had already called for a search warrant. Earl had come back from making a phone call and handed Brege a paper with an address for Franks, courtesy of his friend in the FBI. Brege was delighted, saying they now had two places to visit. He called for backup and said we'd hit McKinley first.

Earl went off with Brege saying we were on our own, Buck and I followed everyone out and got back to our rental and we stopped. "You can start the car for me." I smiled at Buck, he smiled, "Like hell I will, you go drive it over here and I'll get in."

"Let's both take a risk and get moving." I said and we got in and I held my breath as I turned on the ignition. The engine started and we were still alive.

We drove out and followed the caravan of cops and the SWAT van, arriving at the building, where we found two unmarked cars waiting for us. One of the OCU Detectives on the scene said they had an anonymous call from some disgruntled hooker who said she once worked for McKinley and she gave us the address. He checked with the doorman, showed a picture and were told McKinley came in this morning and hasn't left.

Earl winked at Buck and me and said to not get killed. They all entered the lobby, some men went off to the stairway, and the rest went up in the elevator. Buck and I went up the stairs.

Everyone got off on the fifth floor and up to the door that they were told McKinley was in. Brege came up and banged on the door, doing the standard open up, police. There was no answer so they brought over the ram and smashed the door in. Everyone filed in and found a man lying on the kitchen floor, bleeding from a wound in his shoulder. Brege yelled for an EMS and they checked him, he was alive. Another officer came in and said they found two other men in a bedroom, both dead from gunshots.

Buck and I stood out in the hallway, but could see through into the kitchen where the man laid. Earl came out and said that none of the men was McKinley, the doorman must have not seen him leave or he got out another way. The police were knocking on doors in the hallway and asking people if they heard any noises, the gun must have been silenced. The EMS came up shortly and took the wounded man out. Brege came out and said that the man had told him McKinley shot them before leaving the apartment.

"The guy said McKinley had plane reservations to Hong Kong, where his investors were. Chinese are getting into crime here too now. You'd think lead paint would have been enough to kill people, now they are trying to muscle into organized crime." Brege shook his head and watched as the coroner took out the men who didn't make it.

"I got men going to Kennedy Airport; they'll work with airport security and nab him. He ain't leaving town on my watch."

**

Chapter 28

Marina was overjoyed to see Ron and so was Francis. She hadn't seen her nephew in about ten years and welcomed him into her house.

"Aunty Fran, it's so good to see you again. Wow, it's been ages, how are you doing?" He exclaimed as they hugged.

"I'm fine, how's my sister Anna?" she asked.

"Mom is doing as best as she can. Since her Alzheimer's has progressed, she's not very active and the home I have her in is wonderful for taking care of her. Thanks for the financial help you've been giving; it's so good of you." Ron responded.

"Well, I take care of my little sister, even if we can't be together. She and I had that falling out years ago, she didn't like being part of the family and we would argue about it. She was headstrong and left. You haven't told her I was helping financially did you?"

"No, you asked me not to say anything so I didn't. Besides her memory isn't what it used to be." Ron replied.

"Good, now come meet my new husband, you'll like him." Francis took Ron and Marina out to the garden again and did the introductions.

~~*~~

Police were at Kennedy Airport standing at the boarding ramp of the United flight to Hong Kong, waiting for McKinley to show up, and he did. He wasn't very friendly and gave the police a hard time at the airport, to the point they finally had to Taser him. They had him in custody and on his way back to Midtown, to face Brege and the DA.

Brege got off the phone and said "Vice was howling about us taking their case from them, they say now that they had the clubs under surveillance and were ready to move in on them, I said that was bull shit and they were humping the goat on it. Captain Holland from vice wants us to turn over what we have on the clubs and our witness to cooperate with them. No friggin way. I'm taking it to the commissioner about this crap and they ain't getting diddle. I'll cut everyone loose before I turn this over to vice. Assholes!"

I felt that Brege was a little pissed. I wasn't going to turn Marina over to anyone but Brege and the DA. She would not be lost in the system of bureaucratic mire, allowing her to be exposed to her murder. Damon already said he thought there was something going on in Vice and now we had to fight them for lead on this. No way.

I turned to Buck and said, "We are going to need to be on our toes about this. Marina isn't going anywhere except underground if they get pissy about it. It's strange to say, but I'm glad she's with the mob. They can make anyone vanish."

"You think we need to warn Angelo about this?" Buck asked.

"It wouldn't hurt, but let's see who wins the tug of war first."

Strip Club Murders

While we stood there, three men in suits came in and Brege came around his desk and came face to face with the lead man.

"Holland, what the hell you think you're doing. We nailed this case and you can't force your way into it just because you screwed up." Brege said loudly.

"Brege, it was our case before your underhanded stunt of having outsiders case the clubs, prostitution is our jurisdiction, you know that full well." Holland yelled back just as loud.

"We got jurisdiction over organized crime and every damn thing involved with it. In this case, it covers all the Rex Erotica clubs, prostitution, and human trafficking. Shall we call in the FBI and let them have a slice? They've already been here and talked to me about it, where were you during all this, sitting on your haunches and baying at the moon?"

Holland just stared at Brege and then quietly said, "This isn't over. We will get everything from you, count on it." He turned and took his men and walked away.

Earl said to Buck and me "What we have here is a failure to communicate."

Brege came to us and smiled, "The reference to the FBI got a rise out of him."

Bob Moats

Earl said, "Since Marina was kidnapped and taken across state lines, maybe my friend in the Bureau could put her under their protective custody, if we knew where Jim has hiding her." He said knowing full well where she was, but not letting on.

"And I'm not telling." I said simply.

"Let's not get our underwear in a bunch, this will all work out, it's just a tactic to make Holland and his cronies look like their asses are covered. Okay, we got McKinley coming in and he's the rep from Rex Erotica here in the states, but we now believe there are other foreign interests in the whole scam. We can't touch the Chinese connection, but we can shut them down from here."

"My worry isn't so much with the Rex Erotica, but now I'm concerned about the connection with Vice. Someone may have been raking in mucho bucks to look away. I'm betting on Holland right now." I said. "They could get dangerous."

Brege looked like he was a bit on edge, "I'll be talking to Damon about his investigation of Vice, but we may have to step on a few toes ourselves. This whole thing stinks right now and we should be celebrating. Damn." He went to his desk and sat picking up the phone.

Earl looked at us and said, "Anyone for machine food?" He said and we went to the cafeteria and got sandwiches and pop from the machines. We sat and were eating as we watched the people milling about in the room. We were making small talk about nothing in particular, then Earl asked about our visit to the mob hideout.

"It's hardly a hideout. Think Playboy mansion meets CIA. This place is a citadel and has all the conveniences of modern tech with heavy firepower. For a low-key crime syndicate, as Brege called them, they are very concerned for their safety." I said.

"Well, with two mob families merging, Francis Mangelo and Gino Traviano, there's twice the threats from other families. No one wants war, but they are always on edge about turf rights. Even in Detroit, there's a minor mob family there, but there is a strong contingent of African-American gangs running the illegals from Detroit to the suburbs. They don't want anyone poking their noses in on their business. It keeps us hopping."

"I think the bikers have it right, they enjoy sex and drugs and leave everyone else out of it." Buck offered as he sat back trying to force down another bite of the sandwich he had. "Couldn't we have gone out to eat, this stuff tastes like road kill gone worse."

"I'm going to call out to Angelo and see how everyone is getting along. And I have to check in with my lovely wife, who I miss having sex with rather than be here, and see how she is doing." I said as I stood and went to a table off the corner of the room for privacy.

The phone rang about four times until Angelo answered. "Yea, Angelo here."

"Hey Angelo, its Jim, just calling to see if everyone is playing nice out there."

"Oh, we are doin' real good. We got everyone out havin' a BBQ. Care to join us?"

"I'm a bit tied up here with all the crap they got going. Just wanted to give you a heads up that NYPD Vice may be into a bit of corruption and they want Marina to come in a testify for them, but we aren't going to let that happen. I think they don't want her doing so. It's not in their best of interest. Keep an extra careful eye on her. I'll call later to check in and let you know how things are going. Take care." Angelo said the same and we hung up.

I dialed Penny and since it was afternoon now, she should be finished with her show and back at the house. It rang twice and she answered, "You better be on your way back right about now," came the warning.

I was trying not to laugh, "Gosh, I'm glad you can't reach me right now since I'm still in New York. I'd fear for my nether regions if you could grab on."

"Better believe it buster. I'm trying to keep my horny factor in check but you will be in real trouble when you do get back." I could tell she was smiling by the tone in her voice, any other tone and I would worry.

"How's our baby doing?" I asked.

"Willy has forgotten who his daddy is and I've been showing him pictures of Brad Pitt and telling him that's his father. You probably will get bit on the ankles when you come back, so be careful."

"You know, you are one nasty woman when you want to be."

"Remember that Sweetie. So how's it going out there?"

I told her all the gory details and then she said when my case was over, she wanted to go back out to New York to see Francis and interview her since she said it was all right. I said that was fine with me and I'd asked her again to be sure.

"Aren't you going to ask me what I'm wearing?" She inquired.

"No, because that will just make it hard for me to concentrate."

"Or just make it hard for you?"

"Yes, you do have a mean streak. I'm hanging up now before you say something I'll regret." I hung up before she could reply and sat back thinking of her body next to mine, damn.

**

Chapter 29

I came back over to Buck and Earl. "Everything good back in paradise?" Earl asked.

"Penny is having sex withdrawals, and I'm stuck with you two. What are we doing now, so I can keep my mind off Penny?"

"All we can do is wait till McKinley is processed and taken to interrogation. If Holland doesn't get in the way." Earl replied.

Brege came into the makeshift lunchroom and found us. "We need Marina back here, the DA said that we can take her testimony by video, claiming she is in danger and needs protection. They can run the video at the trial to nail McKinley."

Strip Club Murders

"Can't you just turn the prostitution part over to Vice and still take down Rex Erotica?" I asked.

"Sounds simple, but just running strip clubs won't get him any time, kidnapping and prostitution will. We need those clubs to show how he was spreading it out in the city. Just too bad we have only one girl to testify. Having more women sure would make a difference."

One of Brege's men came running in and up to him, "Captain, just got word that the officers bringing in McKinley were high-jacked by three unsubs and they took McKinley. The officers are all right, but one of them said there was something wrong with the hit. He's coming in now."

Brege looked like a man on his last nerve. "Son of a bitch," he roared, "This is not what I expected. This is getting tiresome. I hate this job." He fumed as he stomped out of the room. Earl, Buck and I followed and stood nearby his desk until the officer came in. He looked more worried about Brege than he did having been jumped by thugs.

Brege said calmly, "Davis, I don't blame you for what happened; we're up against the odds, now talk to me."

Davis was told to sit and then he spoke, "We had McKinley in the car coming from the airport. We were driving out and on to Van Wyck Expressway, but just as we hit the on-ramp this SUV ran us up the embankment, our car flipped and we were upside down. Three men came over, pulled the back door open, and dragged McKinley out. I tried to shoot but they started blasting the car. It was odd, they could have killed all of us but they just laid down distracting fire and ran off. I swear, Captain, they were dressed too nicely for hitmen too, I'd bet my pension to say they reminded me of cops."

Brege's eyes went wide and his nostrils flared, I figured he counted to ten, then he calmed and said to one of his other men to get Holland on the phone.

The detective held the phone out and told Brege he had Holland coming on, Brege grabbed the phone and waited, then, "Holland you know why I'm calling, you sleazy hairball, you were behind the grabbing of McKinley from us, nearly killing my men, and I'll have your badge as soon as I prove it." Brege went quiet listening, "Well, we will play that game; I'll take you and McKinley down for this!" He slammed the phone down.

He looked to me and said, "We need Marina's video testimony now. We can take McKinley's henchmen to trial and implicate McKinley as a fugitive. Make it work, Jim."

"I'm sorry Captain, the way things are going here, I don't want her anywhere near this precinct with vice running loose. Ask the DA if the video can be made where the girl is at? I'd agree to working under those terms."

Brege said he couldn't see any reason why they couldn't do that and went off to get Damon in the phone. Earl came to me and asked, "You think don Traviano is going to let the cops stomp all over his property?"

"No, just you, me, Buck, the DA and his recorders are going to go make our feature film, they don't call me C.B. Demille for nothing. Excuse me while I make the arrangements." I walked to where I had some privacy and called Angelo. I gave him the rundown and he said it should be no problem; in fact, he liked the idea of Marina not leaving the property. I said I'd arrange it on this end, if he could call me and let me know when we can come out. Time was getting short; he said he was on it.

I came back to Earl and Buck; Brege had finished his call and came over, "Jim, Damon says it's a go for what you want, it's not the first time he's had to be flexible on these matters."

I said good and I asked Brege for a favor, he and I went off and I told him what I wanted. He agreed.

In another hour, Angelo called and said it was all arranged with don Traviano's blessing and he liked the idea also. I was ready with Buck and Earl, then the DA came in with a rather huge cop, who I found out was a court bailiff who would swear Marina in, and a woman with the video equipment. She looked like she could handle the three boxes of equipment, as she was a bit muscular. Brege escorted us down to a parking garage behind the precinct and there were four big black Chevy Suburbans, with very dark tinted windows. The SUV's all sat in a row and Brege said we could take the end one. I said thanks but took my team to the second one from the left and we loaded everything in. Brege had a tech from electronics sweep the vehicle for bugs or trackers and drivers for the other three cars got in their vehicles and we were ready.

I signaled the driver of the first vehicle and he headed out with me and the rest coming up the rear. All four cars took different directions and I headed south away from where we were going but with a good number of twists and turns down various streets, we were on the way back North to our destination. Buck and Earl were in the back watching out for any tails we may have picked up and they were happy with our progress.

We arrived at the Traviano property and were let in the gate. Angelo came out and greeted us, then we were escorted into a small guesthouse off the side of the main house and found Marina, Ron, Francis and Gino sitting in the small living room. Before I entered the house I noticed a number of rather large men near the guesthouse carrying MP-5 submachine guns, they weren't fooling around.

Gino stood and welcomed me again and I introduced everyone to him. Gino eyed the big cop and I explained he was a court bailiff and would swear Marina in for the video to make it official. He smiled and shook the cop's hand then sat back down.

Mark Damon explained what was going to happen with the taping and had the woman set up her equipment. He took Marina and sat her in an easy chair in front of the camera and told her to relax, it wouldn't hurt a bit. Marina smiled and said she was ready.

Mark sat next to Marina and told the tech woman to start. He looked very legal and spoke as the camera ran. He explained to the camera that this witness had been kidnapped and subjected to unspeakable torture and drugs only to be turned out as a prostitute before being rescued by agents acting through the NYPD. He signaled to the bailiff who swore Marina in using the bible he brought and Marina agreed. Mark started the interview, asking Marina to go back to Detroit, when she worked at the Side Door and continue from there. Marina told of how she came out of the club late one night and was grabbed by three men, the same who were coming into the club looking for women to work at Heaven's Gate. Mark would stop her occasionally and ask a question or two to clarify her statements and then she got to the place where she was held in Detroit and then taken out to New York and her ordeal in the city. She told of when she arrived at the building here, there were about ten other girls there, and McKinley came to the room they were being held, and warned them to cooperate and don't give them any trouble. He opened the door and they brought in a young girl struggling against the men. McKinley told us that she had refused to cooperate and he took out a gun and shot her in the head. They took her out and he said that would happen to us if we didn't do what they said. There was blood everywhere and they left it that way.

I heard Gino say something quietly in Italian, he didn't look pleased.

The taping went on for another hour, Mark asking questions and Marina explaining. Finally, he was happy with the taping and said he had everything he would need to submit the tape into evidence. The tech woman packed her equipment as Gino and Francis were talking to their guests.

"I understand you are an acquaintance of my nephew Ron?" Gino asked Earl.

"Yes, I've come in contact with him in the past. He was very helpful during a murder investigation I was conducting." Earl replied.

"Thank you for helping with this horrible crime, I'll remember you. I sincerely hope this McKinley is convicted, otherwise he is dead to me." Earl felt a chill as Gino nodded at him and said he had work to do and then smiled at Buck and me and went out of the room being followed by two large men. Earl whispered to me, "Out of all the bad guys I've crossed paths with in the world, I'm now a friend of a mob capo, I guess I like it."

Francis came up to the DA and asked if Marina was still needed to do anything in regards to the case, Mark said the video should be enough. They'd hide her identity and her location as a protected witness. Francis said that was acceptable and I gathered my little group so we didn't overstay our welcome. Francis pulled me aside and asked if I had talked to Penny lately and I said I had and Penny was more than happy to interview Francis for her show. Francis loved the idea again and said to let her know when, I said I would.

We headed back to Midtown, happy with the events of the afternoon.

**

Chapter 30

On the way back Mark Damon said to me from his seat in the front, "I've had to try and put away a number of godfathers in my time, that's the first one I actually liked."

"You either like him, or else." I said.

We arrived at Midtown and Mark and his crew went off to go back to their offices. We went in and found Brege. He didn't look happy. I thought what now.

"Two of the other Suburbans were followed and had a bit of a skirmish with one. We got the men in the tail car, they aren't saying a word." Brege said. "You guys lucked out, I hope."

"They seem to be worried about us getting close to wrapping up this case." Earl spoke as he sat on the window ledge.

"Yeah, we just keep getting hit on this. I'm waiting for an all-out assault on the precinct." Brege wasn't smiling.

I asked, "Any more problems from Holland and vice?"

Strip Club Murders

"Strangely not since McKinley was taken, I don't know what good it does for them to have him, he's wanted for a whole boat load of crimes. They can't set him back up; they are screwed if they expect to get any more money from him." Brege started to smile again.

"Maybe they know McKinley can implicate them in his business doings." I offered.

"That's a good point; keep him from spilling the beans. He probably wind up dead now." Earl said.

"Well, there's nothing more you guys can do for us now, I thank you for all your work and I'm sure the city will have some kind of crappy little citation for all of you." He was really smiling now.

We said our good-byes and left Midtown, hopefully for good. It was now just after 5 P.M. so we went back to our hotel suite and I said I wanted to crash for a bit and went in to the bedroom. Earl and Buck turned on the TV and sat watching some game show. I lay on the bed and I could smell Marina's scent on the sheets. It smelled good; it helped me nap.

Around 6:00 by my watch, I heard a phone ring; it was coming from Earl's phone. I laid there listening to the muffled conversation and Earl came into the bedroom, not smiling. I thought, not again.

"Well, I was right, McKinley was found dead in a dumpster down in Queens. Brege still has two of McKinley's associates who can give their testimony in exchange for protection; he has them under extra guard," Earl said.

"Yea, but who's guarding the guards?" I asked.

Earl smiled and said, "There's not many people left in this mess to convict."

Earl went back out to the living room, as I just laid there pretending I was back home. Maybe tomorrow. After I started to drift off again, my cell phone rang, I just wasn't going to get a nap. I answered and it was Mark Damon. I sat up when I heard his voice, he sounded upset.

"What's wrong?" I asked.

"Jim, we just found the woman who took the videos, she was knocked out, and the tape we took is gone. You had better warn the Travianos to watch Marina closely. Just a warning." He said.

I thanked him and went out to the main room and told Buck and Earl about the call. Earl said they are really trying to make this all disappear. I said I had to call Angelo and I went back to the bedroom.

Angelo came on the phone and I told him about the tape and McKinley, he growled about the way this was going. I said to keep a close eye on Marina since it seems someone wants all the evidence to go away. He said he would and we hung up. I was getting hungry so went out and asked if they wanted to go get something to eat. Buck spoke first and said he'd like a nice big steak, Earl just said a burger would be fine with him.

We went out to the Charger, since I had returned the rental, left the Hilton, found a nice restaurant, and went in to eat. We were seated and ordered, then made small talk until our food came. Buck got his steak and Earl got his burger, I took fish and chips. We sat for about an hour relaxing then went out around 7:30. We had just gotten to the Charger when my cell phone rang; it was Angelo.

"Mr. Richards, we got a problem. Ron and Marina decided they wanted to go shopping for some women stuff and I sent a couple men with them. Well, they got jumped at the local mall, Reggie's okay, but they got Marina. Gino's pissed and has his men out looking for them. I don't know what you can do, just wanted to let you know." He said.

"Okay, keep me informed. Thanks and talk later." I hung up. "Shit."

"What's wrong?" Buck asked.

"They got Marina." I told them what Angelo said to me. "Where would they take her?" I dialed Brege and he came on, I related the details to him, he swore and I asked if he could think of any place they would take her. He had no idea; they killed McKinley so it would be the most likely option for the girl. I was getting pissed myself now, and asked if he thought that Vice may have a safe house they use or some building somewhere? Brege said they had a number of places, but it would take too long to track them down. I thought for a minute and it came to me that McKinley's secretary said they had a warehouse near their offices were they kept the porn videos. I asked Brege if his men had checked it out. He said they did, but found little there other than a lot of boxes of porn and the room where they temporarily kept the kidnapped girls. I asked him for the address and he dug it out. I thanked him and checked the address on my Palm and we drove there.

We arrived and found four cars parked by the building. By a large opened bay door, there was a truck and a couple of men loading boxes of what I presumed were videos into the truck. I said it looks like we need reinforcements. Earl pulled his phone and called Brege explaining that we hadn't found the girl but there was a lot of activity at the warehouse. Brege said not to get involved until he got there with backup. We sat watching and then a van pulled up and three men got out dragging Marina. I wanted to go in shooting, but Earl said there were probably more men inside than we could handle so we should wait. I said the hell with waiting; at least we can check through the windows, they may kill her before help comes.

Earl got out of the car followed by Buck and we snuck over to the building; there didn't seem to be any surveillance around and no guards. We went to the windows and looked in. I couldn't see anyone so we moved around the building and found windows looking into a back room where we saw Holland and about six men standing around with Marina now tied to a chair. We couldn't hear them but they were arguing. Holland pointed to Marina and the man standing next to her pulled out his weapon and aimed it at Marina.

Earl pulled out his gun and shot through the window taking out the man. I could see his head explode and he dropped down hard. The rest of the men in the room panicked and everyone was ducking for cover. Earl shot another man attempting to shoot Marina, as I had busted the window in front of me and was blasting away at anything that moved. Buck found a door just down the way from us and went in. I saw Buck in the room off the side and went to look for the door and went in, followed now by Earl.

We were moving carefully between the shelves of videos as Buck and the men were still firing at each other. I saw Marina near the end of one stack, I ran and grabbed her chair and pulled her back while Earl gave me cover fire. I pulled her to the back of the building, took out my pocketknife, and cut her loose.

214

Bob Moats

I found a small closet that contained cleaning equipment and told her to go in there and stay until I came for her. Earl and Buck were still firing and I could hear sirens now approaching. Damn, about time, my ammo was running low even though I brought another clip this trip.

The men must have heard the sirens and they started to bolt for the exits. The cars pulled up as they were coming out of the building and a couple of the bad guys thought they could shoot it out, but there were more cops than bad guys. Brege came around his car wearing a vest that made him look even bigger than he was. Earl, Buck and I came up behind the men still firing, I saw Holland head off the side and disappear.

Outside the firing ceased, they must have gotten the situation under control. Brege came in the building through the open bay door and I yelled and pointed the direction that Holland went. He took a couple of his men and went that way as we watched the cops round up and cuff the perps.

I remembered Marina and ran back to get her from the closet, she was sitting on the floor shaking, I helped her up and she clung tightly to me still shaking. I told her it was all right and it was finally over. I brought her back through the shelves to where everyone was and Earl gave me a smile, then got a strange look as his eyes drifted past me. I turned and saw Holland standing between the shelves with his gun pointed at Marina. Earl couldn't shoot since Marina and I were in the way and I had put my gun in its holster. Holland fired at Marina and all I could do was jump in front of her hoping for the best. Another couple of shots were made, coming from Brege shooting Holland from behind him.

Everyone ran to me as I lay on the ground feeling the pain in my chest where I presumed the bullet went in. Damn, I didn't have my vest this time.

**

Chapter 31

It was dark but I could see. My eyes were closed but I could see. I saw the love of my life, Penny, on my right, sitting by my hospital bed holding my hand. I couldn't feel it. I saw Buck sitting in his usual stretched out position on a chair to my left. I wanted to kick at his feet as I always did to him in my office lobby, but my legs wouldn't move. Matter of fact, I couldn't move any part of my body. I was lying on the bed and I had no idea why I was there, and why Penny and Buck were starting to fade out. I could hear a small sound coming from my right, it was a beeping noise, like you hear in those hospital shows where the patient was hooked up to a heart monitor.

Bob Moats

Was I hooked up to a heart monitor and was that noise coming from my vitals? The room was getting darker now and the beeping was starting to fade as well.

Then I thought I heard Penny talking in my ear, saying that she was still horny and I had better wake up to take care of her, or else. I was now hearing her words and I was seeing a number of naked Pennys floating over my bed. I had to wake up. I slowly opened my eyes and Penny gave out a cry causing Buck to stir from his chair and sit up. Penny ran to the door and called for the nurses and they all came in making a fuss over me. I was looking at everyone still not sure what the hell was going on. Then it started to come back to me. I was shot.

The nurses were all checking my vitals and I could see Penny standing at the end of my bed waving at me like I had just returned from a trip on a train. Buck was standing next to her now, grinning that walrus smile of his, and doing the stupid wave also. I closed my eyes again when they flashed a light in them and I brought my hand up to shield my eyes from the light. The nurse was stronger than I was at the moment and pulled my hand away and forcibly open my eye to flash the light again. I guess my pupils were responsive so she stopped blinding me. A doctor finally came in and was doing the same things the nurses did, why do they even bother with doctors I wondered.

Strip Club Murders

Buck went out of the room and came back with a whole slew of people. Earl came in first followed by Ron and Marina, then Brege and then Francis and Angelo. A second or two later, Gino walked in and came to my bedside and whispered in my ear, "Anything you need, it's yours. You did good." He smiled and went to stand by his wife. Penny was just about jumping on me and I asked hoarsely if she could stop that. She smiled and sat quietly on the bed next to me.

Brege came around and said the city of New York wants to give me a commendation for my heroics and quick thinking. I said I wasn't thinking, just acting on adrenaline.

"Whatever, we gathered up Holland's men and they are all singing like birds. Holland was trying to recoup his losses when Rex Erotica was crumbling by taking the inventory of porn to sell on the black market to China. He knew if we got McKinley to trial it would come out he was involved, along with a number of his own men. He was trying to cover everything up by taking out all the people who could finger him or keep the case alive. Commissioner's not happy and is ordering a full-blown investigation into Vice. You and your friends sure stirred up some trouble here. I may retire happy now."

Earl came over and said he was thinking about making me an honorary black ops agent. I said to keep it; this is too much work already. Marina came to me, planted a big kiss on my cheek, and thanked me for saving her.

I looked to Penny and asked, "I presume I'm still in New York, when did you get here?"

"Yesterday morning, Gino and Francis sent their private jet to bring me to New York, and then they picked me up and brought me here."

"Yesterday? How long have I been here?"

"Two nights and a day, they said they didn't know if you would make it, the bullet just missed hitting your heart, but did mess up a bit of your insides. They worked on you most of yesterday." She kissed me on the cheek and continued, "Francis and Gino have said they are paying for your entire hospital expenses."

I smiled and thanked everyone for their kindness and help. The doctor wasn't sure if he wanted to bother don Traviano, but did say I needed my rest now. Everyone said good-bye and filed out. The doctor said Penny could stay. Earl said he extended the room at the Hilton and he and Buck would be there.

Penny smiled and said, "I had a nice talk with Marina, and she told me the whole story from her perspective. You did good for her. I guess I understand when you tell me your reasons for staying in this business; I could see how happy she was to be out of all the trouble. I don't approve of getting shot though, so stop that, or wear your vest all the time on a case."

I said, "I will, just for you, now am I well enough to have some hospital sex?" She smiled and said to rest, later on the sex.

About a month later, Penny, Buck and I returned to New York, for a special occasion now, Marina and Ron were getting married. The wedding was going to be on Gino and Francis' property, and we had driven all the way out in my new Lincoln Town Car that was delivered to me last week, with a card from the Traviano's saying thanks. I was in heaven behind the wheel. I almost had Buck drive Penny and I out like he did in the limo for the magic convention, but I wanted the thrill of driving it. Buck said he'd drive it back and I agreed. We arrived at the estate and through the gate up to the house. Penny had been here before when she was given a guest room in the house back when she was brought out while I was in the hospital, and she said she wanted a house just like this. I said to save her money.

Angelo came out to greet us and I was surprised to see Earl follow him out. We all shook hands and we were taken to our rooms where we would stay for a couple of days. Penny had arranged to interview Francis, and Gino even agreed to an interview also. Lonie was coming out with her film crew in two days for the taping and Penny had announced on her show about the event.

"So are you part of the family now?" I asked Earl.

"I got an invite last week, it surprised me, then Ron asked me to be his best man, that surprised me even more." he smiled.

"Yea, he asked me and I turned him down, so you were the second choice." I said jokingly. "That's all right that you are best man, but I was asked by Marina to give her away, I told her I was honored, but I thought she should ask Gino, and she did. I'm still a little off my mark from the bullet in my chest so I don't want to strain myself. Penny was asked to be the bride's maid, so don't get any ideas about hooking up, I will be watching."

Earl smiled and held his closed fist out, I wondered what he was doing and he said to hold my hand out. I did and he dropped a bullet in my hand and said he got it from Brege after they took it from the hospital. It's the one that almost took me out. I looked at it and said, "Amazing how such a little thing can do so much damage."

We all got ready for the big event and later the wedding went well. We partied the night away and when everyone was resting later that night, I took the bullet out of my pocket and showed it to Penny. I told her what it was and said now I have another plaque to put on my office wall.

THE END

For every ending, there's a new beginning.

Preview of the next Book,

"Made-for-TV Murders"

I was sitting quietly in my office one morning when Hollywood walked in.

Okay, to explain, we need to go back just over a year, when I first became involved in the classmate murders, or more correctly, cheerleader murders. I became involved in the hunt for two serial killers who were stalking and killing the cheerleaders from my old high school, although forty years later. The first cheerleader murdered was an old childhood flame that I knew when I was in eighth grade, I hadn't seen her in over forty years and she turned up strangled in her shower, while the police were watching her. Well, not actually watching her in the shower, but while she was in protective custody. Then four more aging, former cheerleaders were murdered while in protective custody, which drove homicide detective Will Trapper just about nuts. He was the primary investigator on the case back then, and I became a bug in his attempts to find the killers. We did finally track down and took out the killers, and Penny was the last of the cheerleaders and the only one to survive. Happily for me.

After the basic story was released to the national media, I had decided to sit at my laptop and write the whole detailed account into a novel, so I spent a year, on and off, putting it all down into book form that I finally finished about two months ago. I had found a few contacts in the industry and managed to find a book agent to finally get around to reading the thing. Funny thing is the media, news, television, blogs and such had spread the story about the crazed killers and their leader, who all ended up dead, leaving a female Detroit TV talk show hostess as the last unharmed victim, so my book was very relevant. It was finally published.

Before I even started writing the book, the story released by the media was big, and back then we had been approached by a few TV network producers who wanted to put the whole incident into a mini-series movie for television, but nothing ever came of it. Mostly because the producers needed everyone involved to allow their part in the story to be told. There were a few holdovers on giving permission to have them portrayed, but then when my book came out; it was now a way to film the story based on the book. It's amazing what you can write about people as long as you don't mention real names without permission. But back then the movie it wasn't a go project. Until today.

So when my office door flew open on that morning and in strode three men in suits, I thought the FBI was invading my space. The lead man held out a card, which I took carefully and gazed at the name and company, James Drury, Really Big Show Pictures.

"I presume you are Mr. Richards, Jim Richards?" He spoke as his two followers stood quietly by.

"I am, and what can I do for you?" I replied, hoping from seeing the Really Big Show Pictures printed on the card, they were here to talk book options for a film.

"As you see from my card, I'm with a film production company and we want to talk to you about your book, Classmate Murders." He answered my thoughts.

I was already spending my film residuals on a villa in the Barbados, "I'm listening." I said simply, so not to queer the deal. "Please have a seat." I motioned to the client chairs, they sat, the lead man, Drury, at the front chair, his henchmen sat back by the wall on my extra chairs. They had a grim look to them, must be the Michigan weather after a life on the sunny west coast.

"Mr. Richards, you not only wrote the book about the two serial killers, but you also lived it. I'm impressed. My company directors have sent me to see if we can come to some agreement, so we can put your ordeal on film, which will be presented on the Lifetime Network. It will be a made for television mini-series. Have you been approached by any other production companies?" he said with a smile on his face, looking like a vulture waiting for the soon to be carcass to make its last gasp.

"I haven't had the pleasure yet to be set about by the industry, you are the first." I smiled back, trying to keep from becoming a carcass.

"Have you considered the film usage of your book?" He never broke the smile, his lips barely moving while he talked, reminding me of a ventriloquist.

"It has crossed my mind." Several times in fact.

"We are authorized to talk a deal with you for the rights to put your book to film, and I hope we can come to some arrangement." he spoke like a lawyer. I wasn't fond of lawyers, I'd rather he talk like a guy sitting in a bar talking to me about the weather.

"Mr. Drury, cut to the chase, what is the deal, and how much control will I have over the script writing?" I had heard horror stories about authors' books being taken to film and butchered. I was stunned to watch the TV movie of a Robert Parker book about Police Chief Jesse Stone, the movie had very little in comparison with the book other than the title and character names. "As you know Classmate Murders is a true story, it's not good to fool with the truth, or embellish it to make it exciting. The whole thing as I lived it was exciting, and scary, as it played out. It would make a good film as is. Just how much of a say would I have in the production of the thing?"

"Well, we are open for your input, after all you were there. We could bring you on as technical advisor as well as the story author. I'm sure you would need to be on hand while our writers would put the story into a screenplay, to keep the authenticity of it intact. I'm sure we could even give you a producing credit."

They were throwing me a bone to get me to give in. "As technical advisor, how much weight would my voice have in the scheme of things. I would make a suggestion and the director would say that's nice, but we'll do it his way. I don't want the thing to turn into some director's vision of the story, he or she wasn't there."

Drury was quiet for a bit, "You are quite right Mr. Richards. I'm impressed as to your integrity of the incident."

"It was very personal to me, I had friends die terrible deaths and I was almost killed to boot. I want the film to show that terror that was felt by all concerned." I said.

Drury was silent again, then took a breath and spoke, "I do hope we can come to some agreement, I really enjoyed your book, I did read it as I do any book we consider for filming. I can see you would bring an honest eye to it and I'm ready to talk options."

I stood and went to my office door, I hung out the sign saying I was not available; I had a number of signs for my actions, and locked the door. I came back to my chair and said. "Let's talk."

For the next two hours, we haggled about what they wanted and what I wanted for the production of my book. I had a producing credit that I insisted was more than just honorary; I had to have a say in the thing. He agreed, but with conditions, that the other producers had to be in on the process. I thought that was like saying I was the only Democrat in a room full of Republicans, who wins? We talked about how the book would be transformed into script and I wanted my say about what the actors would say and how the plot went along, Drury agreed reluctantly. All along, his two assistants were writing down our agreements and conditions and then we came to a final point where we were both happy with everything.

Strip Club Murders

Drury said they would have a contract written up and a check for the rights to their options to the book. I was holding my breath when I thought about the agreed on two hundred grand that they offered. I would have held out for half, I wasn't greedy, but two hundred thousand dollars sounded so much better. I even managed to finagle a percentage of the profits later on when the film was released. Being as it was a made for television movie the profits wouldn't be as great as a theatrical release, but I did manage to get a percentage of the DVD video sales and rentals. I was very happy.

The three men took their leave and departed. I just now had to break the news to Penny, and I could almost see her packing her bags for a round the world vacation.

CONTINUED IN THE BOOK...

~~*~~

Bob Moats

Jim Richards Family of Readers

Thanks to the following people who are now part of the Jim Richards Family of Readers. They have read a book or more and enjoyed them. They all volunteered to be included in the list. If you are a fan of the books, send me your full name and you will be included in future books. Send your name to murdernovels@bobmoats.com to be added here and on the website. (updated 3-30-14)

* Achim Feifel * Al Norris * Alex Wheatley * Alexandra Delporte-Wilkinson * Amy Tapia * Andrea Bryan * Anne Shepherd * Arianda Sugar * Arlene Markowski * Ashley Augustus * Audra Hall * Barbara Hughes * Barbara Sammons * Barbara Schuler * Barbara Zirger * Beth Donohue Plenskofski * Betsy Childress * Beth Gibson * Bill Sandy * Bill Tornquist * Billie-jo Collie * Boni J Rychener * Carl Bishopric * Carla Lewis * Carole Henderson * Carolyn Conroy * Carolyn Riddle-Linington * Cassy Bailey * Chad Hudson * Charlotte L Duran * Cheryl L. Everett * Cindy Ackley Nunn * Cindy Valstad * Connie Bancroft * Corinne Kay O'Daniel * Dana Robbins Chuchran * Dana Wichita * Danielle Monique * Darren Heald * Dave Travers * David Wilkinson * DeAnn Jannereth * Deanna Miller * Deb Breuker Balbo * Debbie Carter * Debbie White * Deborah Fartuch * Deborah Gauze * Deborah Sullivan * Dee King * Denise Freeman * Diana Carver * Dixie Beck * Donna Gould * Donna Thompson * Donny Minter * Doris Kight * Eddie Moore

Strip Club Murders

* Eric Walters * Felicia Annette Bradfield * Francine Menor * Gail Chesney * Georgiann Minster * George Conner * Greg Colucci * Hayley Rankin * Harold Garcia * Heidi Arnold * Irma Ranee Coy * Jacqueline Moss * Jan Kimball * Janice Schneider * Janice Spoor * Jennifer Redmond * Jessica Keown-Belous * Jim Beck * Jo Boguslaw * Jo Turner * Joanne Marie Turner * John Peiffer * John Wisbiski * Joseph Wauro * Joyce Stacy * Joyce Trifiletti * Judy Franklin * Judy Travers * Judy Padgett * Julie Heath * Junnahvee Benson * Karen Dahl * Karen Grams * Karen Higham * Karen Kaiser * Karen Meinburg Richwine * Karen Kirkman Parker * Karin Hawkins * Karin Vasvari * Kathleen Donohue Roesing * Kathleen Riddle-Wolfe * Kathy Hinds Moore * Kathy Jones * Kathy Mitchell * Katie Benzler * Kay Burns * Kelly Garcia * Ken Boggs * Keota Rodriguez * Kiera Mccarthy * Kim Estes * Kitty Stolle * Kristie Sciler * Kirsty Stanton * LaLonnie Scallen * Larry Morris * Leann Parr * Lenora Scales * Leslie Marie Jackson * Linda Forester * Linda Ingle Cox * Linda Kennerö * Linda Magill * Lisa Bower * Liz Gibson * Lorraine Wiman * Loretta Alexander * Lynda Bowles * Lynette Lawrance * LuAnn Louttit * Manny Rothman * Marcia Gibson DeWitt * Marie Calder * Marlene Bryan * MaryLouise Kramp * Mary Lynn Gross * Megan Atkins * Meghan Hyden * Melody Cannavan * Michael Carruthers * Michael Dinkens * Michael Vannoy * Michelle Burns-Mitchell * Michelle Pilcher * Micki Potter * Mike Moats * Mimi Baur * Myrna Hecht * Nadine Sutton * Natalie Quine * Neena Martin * O'Della Wilson * Pat Pollington * Pat Rohn * Patricia Jarmon * Patricia C Trezza * Patrick Barry * Paul Lawrance * Peggy Davis * Phyllis Bassett * Raylene Matheny * Rebecca Collins Besner * Renee Brumley * Reta Hanna * Reta Moats * Roberta Navarro-Harder * Sally Berneathy * Sally Hubler * Sarah Santos *

Bob Moats

Satka Nikc * Sharon E. Edwards * Sharon Mangini *
Sharon McMillon * Sheena Rawl * Sherry Amstutz *
Shirley Alvarez * Shirley Davies * Shirley Williams *
Stacie Rowe * Stephanie Conner * Steve Cullen * Susan
Haughton * Susan Hesse Adams * Susan Salomon *
Suzan K Chase * Taisha Cullum * Tamara Moore *
Tammy Castleberry * Tammy Lynn Wood * Ted Murphy
* Terri Atkins * Terri Creech * Terry Raab * Tonia
Rachael Riggs-Williams * Travis Fleury-Lopez * Twyla
Gawlas * Val Brooks * Walt Munsel * Yvonne Isakson *

Thank you to all these wonderful people.

Thank you for purchasing this book. I hope
you enjoy it as much as I enjoyed writing it
for my faithful readers. Please feel free to
email me to tell me what you thought about
my stories. I love hearing from the readers. I
can be reached at
murdernovels@bobmoats.com thanks again!

*